Dirty Bertie

STINKY STORIES

DAVID ROBERTS WRITTEN BY ALAN MACDONALD

Stripes

Collect all the Dirty Bertie books!

Worms!
Fleas!
Pants!
Burp!
Yuck!
Crackers!
Bogeys!
Fetch!
Fangs!
Kiss!
Ouch!
Snow!
Pong!
Pirate!
Scream!
Toothy!
Dinosaur!
My Joke Book
My Book of Stuff

Contents

STRIPES PUBLISHING
An imprint of Little Tiger Press
1 The Coda Centre, 189 Munster Road,
London SW6 6AW

A paperback original
First published in Great Britain in 2013

ISBN: 978-1-84715-385-2

A CIP catalogue record for this book is available from the British Library.

Printed and bound in the UK.

10 9 8 7 6 5 4 3 2 1

Dirty Bertie

MUD!

For Kate, James and little "O" ~ D R

For everyone at Greythorn
Primary School ~ A M

Contents

MUD!

CHAPTER 1

"BERTIE! HANDS OUT OF YOUR POCKETS!" thundered Miss Boot.

"I'm cold, Miss," moaned Bertie.

"Then run around!"

Bertie made a feeble show of stamping his feet. He hated football practice. Why did Miss Boot have to drag them outside in the freezing cold?

Why couldn't they practise indoors?

Bertie was brilliant at watching football. He was terrific at talking about it. He just wasn't any good at *playing it*. During a game he never seemed to be in the right place. Most of the time he watched the ball zooming back and forward over his head. And when it did come his way everyone yelled advice: "PASS! MOVE IT! CROSS IT!" Bertie dithered – and by the time he made up his mind, the ball was at the other end of the pitch.

Miss Boot started the lesson with some warm-up exercises. She was wearing her bright orange tracksuit, the one which made her look like a giant satsuma. The class dribbled in and out of cones. They passed back and forth. They practised heading the ball without squealing.

After ten minutes, Miss Boot called them together.

"Before we start a game, I have some good news. From this term the Pudsley Junior team has a new coach. Me."

"Hooray!" cheered Know-All Nick.

A lump of mud hit him on the ear. Bertie looked up at the sky and whistled.

"Now, we have an important match on Friday and I am looking for new players," Miss Boot went on. "Who would like to play for the school team?"

A dozen hands shot up. Bertie kept his hands by his sides. He shivered. He tried pulling his shirt down over his knees to keep warm.

"Excellent," said Miss Boot. "And hands up if you want to play in goal?"

No hands went up.

Bertie felt someone pinch his arm.

"YOW!" he cried.

Know-All Nick looked up at the sky.

"Bertie!" said Miss Boot. "Are you volunteering?"

"Me?" said Bertie.

"Yes, have you played in goal before?"

"No, no ... I can't... I don't..."

"He's just being modest, Miss!" said Nick, thumping Bertie on the back. "Ask anyone, he's brilliant!"

"Hmm," said Miss Boot. Brilliant was not a word she connected with Bertie. Surely there had to be someone else?

"What about you, Nicholas?" she said.

"I can't, Miss. I've got weak ankles," simpered Nick.

"Really," said Miss Boot. "Eugene, how about you?"

"Sorry, my mum doesn't like me playing football."

"Trevor?"

"Haven't got any boots, Miss."

Bertie looked around in desperation. Surely *someone* wanted to play in goal?

"That settles it then," sighed Miss Boot. "You are in goal on Friday, Bertie. *DO NOT LET ME DOWN.*"

"But Miss—" began Bertie.

Miss Boot blew a shrill blast on her whistle and bustled off to start the game.

Bertie stared after her. This couldn't be happening. Him playing in goal for the school team? It was a disaster! A nightmare! Bertie had never played in goal in his life, not even in the playground. He didn't know how to save a ball – he couldn't even save his pocket money. That two-faced toad Nick was behind this. He knew very well Bertie was no good at football. He just wanted to see him make a fool of himself.

After the practice, Bertie trudged back to school with Darren, Eugene and Donna.

"Never mind," said Donna. "It wasn't that bad."

"No," said Darren. "When you kept your eyes open you did much better."

Know-All Nick caught up with them. His shirt and shorts were spotless.

"Hey, Bertie, what was the score again? Remind me," he smirked.

Bertie ignored him.

"Six? Or was it seven? I lost count."

"At least Miss Boot won't want me in the team," said Bertie.

"That's where you're wrong," grinned Nick. "There's no one else."

Bertie groaned. "Why me? Can't someone else go in goal?"

"No thanks!" said Darren. "I'm a striker. Anyway, goalies always get the blame when you lose."

"You think we'll lose?" asked Bertie.

"Are you kidding?" said Darren. "We're playing Cropper Lane."

Bertie looked blank.

"They're top of the league," said Donna. "They haven't lost a match."

"HA! HA!" gurgled Nick. "It'll be a thrashing! I'm *definitely* coming to watch. I wouldn't miss this for anything!"

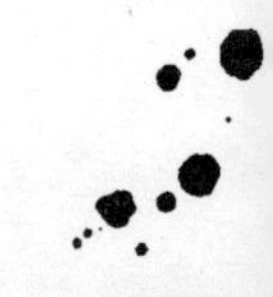

CHAPTER 2

Bertie plodded home after school. Over supper he broke the news to his parents.

"The school team?" said Dad. "That's terrific!"

"Mmm," said Bertie. "Except they want me to play in goal."

"Well that's good, isn't it?" beamed Mum. "You don't look very excited."

"Of course he's excited," said Dad. "I had no idea you played in goal, Bertie."

"I don't!" groaned Bertie. "That's the point. I only got picked by mistake!"

"Don't be silly," said Mum. "You're probably better than you think."

"I'M NOT!" wailed Bertie. "I'm rubbish!"

"Well I'm sure it'll be fine," said Mum. "As long as you do your best no one's going to mind."

Bertie thought Miss Boot would mind. Miss Boot hated losing at anything – even tiddlywinks. If Bertie played badly she'd probably use him as a football and boot him round the pitch.

Dad had fetched his old trainers from the hall. "I used to play football a bit myself," he said. "Just over in the park, but I was pretty good."

"Really?" said Bertie. It was the first he'd heard about it.

"Why don't we have a kick-about in the garden? I could give you a few tips."

Five minutes later, Bertie stood between two flower-pot goalposts. He was wearing his woolly gloves and a baseball cap. Dad bounced the ball a few times and placed it on the lawn.

"Now," he said, "make yourself big. Not like that, crouch down. Arms wide, head up, eye on the ball. Now I'm going to come at you, try to put me off."

Bertie waved his arms. "MISS, MISS, MISS!" he yelled.

"What are you doing?" asked Dad.

"Putting you off."

"Not like that. I mean come out!"

"I thought I was in goal!" said Bertie.

Dad sighed. "Listen. I'll take a shot, you just try and stop it, OK?"

Dad took three steps back. He ran up and thumped the ball with all his might. Bertie watched it sail miles over his head into next-door's garden.

CRASH! TINKLE!

"Whoops," said Dad. "Maybe we'll finish this another time."

The next few days passed in a daze. Bertie couldn't get the football match out of his mind. Even in his sleep he had nightmares about it. He dreamed he was playing against a team of Miss Boots. Miss Boot dribbled. She passed to Miss Boot. Miss Boot shot. Bertie dived…

He woke up on his bedroom floor, cold with sweat.

CHAPTER 3

The day of the big match arrived. Bertie stared at the drops of rain running down the minibus window. He was doomed.

"Cheer up," said Darren. "What's the worst that can happen?"

"We lose," said Bertie. "And I let in twenty goals."

"You won't!" said Darren. "You're not *that* bad."

"No?" said Bertie.

"No!" said Darren. "You're just not very good."

"Thanks," said Bertie. Donna turned round from the seat in front.

"You never know, you might play well," she said. "We might even win."

"Against Cropper Lane?" said Darren.

"Hey, Bertie!" called a loud voice behind them. "Catch!"

Bertie turned round. A toffee hit him on the nose.

"HA! HA!" jeered Know-All Nick. "Call yourself a goalie? You can't catch for toffee!"

The rain fell in buckets as the bus turned into the school drive and came to a halt. The Pudsley Junior team trooped off. They stared at the field. It sloped like the deck of a sinking ship. There were a few tufts of grass – the rest was a sea of mud. A seagull swam in one of the puddles.

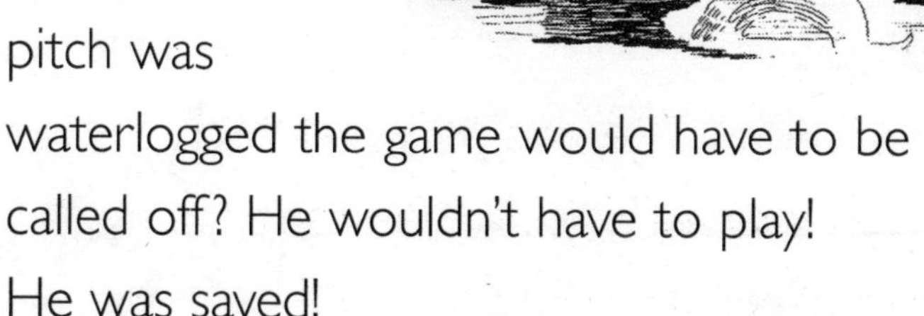

Bertie felt a wave of relief. Surely if the pitch was waterlogged the game would have to be called off? He wouldn't have to play! He was saved!

"Right, hurry up and get changed," barked Miss Boot, putting up her umbrella.

"But Miss, what about the pitch?" said Bertie.

"What about it?"

"It's a bog. We can't play on that!"

"Nonsense! A few little puddles never hurt anyone. In my day we played hockey when the snow was up to our knees!"

Just then the Cropper Lane team ran out in their red shirts. They warmed up, taking it in turns to blast the ball into one of the goals.

Know-All Nick sidled over. "Pretty big aren't they? Look at that number nine. I wouldn't want to get in *his* way." He gave Bertie a sickly smile.

Bertie stomped off to the dressing room to get changed.

CHAPTER 4

SPLODGE, SPLODGE, SPLODGE.

Bertie paddled around in his goalmouth. So far he hadn't let in any goals. Considering they'd been playing for five minutes this was pretty good. He was already rather dirty but that didn't bother him. Bertie loved mud. Adults were always shouting at him to keep out of it.

But goalkeepers were actually *expected* to get muddy. It was part of the job.

Bertie sploshed through a puddle. *I wonder what it's like for mud sliding?* he thought. Taking a run, he skidded across his goal. Mud sprayed everywhere. Not bad. Next he chose the biggest puddle in the goal. This time he skidded right through it.

THUMP! WHOOSH!

Something zoomed past his head. He looked up. Why was everyone cheering? The Cropper Lane players were all crowding round the number nine. Bertie turned his head slowly. A football nestled in the back of the net.

Miss Boot turned crimson.

"BERTIE!" she thundered. "WHAT ARE YOU PLAYING AT?"

"Sorry! I wasn't watching," said Bertie.

Darren picked the ball out of the net.

"You're meant to try and stop it," he grumbled.

"I wasn't ready!" complained Bertie. "Somebody should tell me if they're going to shoot!"

Pudsley Juniors kicked off. Bertie sighed. This was exactly why he hadn't wanted to play in goal. You stood around for ages freezing to death then everyone blamed you for one tiny mistake.

From the touchline Know-All Nick gave him a thumbs-up sign.

"Nice one, Bertie!" he jeered.

For the rest of the half, Bertie tried to focus on the game. It wasn't too hard as most of the action took place around his goal. Cropper Lane were well on top. Pudsley got everyone back and defended grimly. Bertie dived, slipped and sloshed in the mud as shots rained in like hailstones. One crashed off the post. Another thudded off the crossbar. A third squirted through Bertie's legs and was going in until it got stuck in a puddle.

At half-time the Pudsley players trudged off, grateful to be only one goal down. Their coach was not pleased.

"USELESS! PATHETIC!" screeched Miss Boot. "I didn't come all this way to see you lose! Now go out there and get back in this game!"

The second half began. The rain fell in sheets. Bertie got muddier and muddier. His shirt stuck to his back. His shorts were brown. His boots sucked and squelched every time he moved.

Then the miracle happened. Pudsley scored! It was Donna who surprised everyone, ending a mazy dribble by poking the ball home.

"GOAL!" bellowed Miss Boot, waving her umbrella.

"GOAL!" cried Bertie, doing a handstand in the mud.

Know-All Nick shook his head. The Cropper Lane players looked at each other in disbelief. With five minutes left, the scores were level at 1–1.

"Come on, Pudsley!" roared Miss Boot. "You can do it!"

Cropper Lane kicked off. Pudsley cleared the ball, booting it anywhere. From a throw-in the number nine barged his way into the penalty area.

"Come out, Bertie!" yelled Darren.

Bertie tore out of his goal like an express train. He skidded in the mud and couldn't stop... "ARGH!" cried the number nine as Bertie flattened him.

"PEEP!" The referee pointed to the spot for a penalty.

The Pudsley players groaned. Only a few minutes left and Bertie was going to cost them the game.

Bertie picked himself up and splodged back to his goal line. *Typical*, he thought, *now we're going to lose and everyone will blame me.*

He crouched with his hands at the ready. He'd never faced a penalty before.

The number nine pawed the ground. He began his run-up. Bertie heard someone singing loudly behind his goal:

"There's only one Pudsley goalie,

And his pants are all holey…!"

Bertie swung round to see Know-All Nick's grinning face.

THUD! … WHACK!

Something thumped him on the back of the head, sending him sprawling. Half-dazed, Bertie saw a ball bounce in the mud. He reached out to grab it before it could cross the line. Seconds later he was mobbed by his teammates.

"Brilliant, Bertie!"

"What a save!"

"You weren't even looking!"

They crowded round him, slapping him on the back. Bertie grinned and spat out a piece of grass.

Soon after, the whistle blew for the end of the game. The Pudsley players threw their arms in the air. Miss Boot danced in the puddles. A draw against the might of Cropper Lane was as good as a victory. Bertie was carried off the pitch by his cheering teammates. He caught sight of a scowling boy trying to slink away unseen. Bertie scooped a clod of mud off his shirt and took aim...

SPLAT!

CHEESE!

CHAPTER 1

It was twenty to nine. Bertie was late for school.

"Bertie! Hurry up!" yelled his mum.

"I'm not going!"

"Get down here now!" cried Mum. "I'm counting to five."

"The door's stuck! I can't get out!"

Mum folded her arms. "One, two,

three, four ... four and a half..."

The bathroom door burst open and Bertie stomped downstairs.

"At last," said Mum. "Let's have a look at you. There, I think you look very smart."

Bertie stared at his reflection in the hall mirror. He hardly recognized himself. He was wearing a clean white shirt and school tie. His face glowed a healthy pink. His hair had been washed for the first time in months. Instead of resembling a bird's nest, it was neatly combed and parted.

"I look ridiculous," moaned Bertie. "Why can't I dress normally?"

"You know why," replied Mum. "It's the class photo today and I want you to look your best."

Bertie tugged at his tie.

"It's strangling me! I can't breathe!"

"Well you'll have to put up with it," said Mum. "Just for once, I'd like a class photo I can keep."

"But we've got millions of photos of me!" said Bertie.

"Yes and you're pulling a face in all of them."

Bertie sighed. It wasn't his fault his class photos were never any good. Photographers always made the class stand around for ages. It was boring. By the time they did take the photo Bertie had lost interest and was looking the wrong way.

Mum straightened his tie. "Anyway, this year you're going to be smart. And I expect you to stay like this all day."

"OK, I'll try," groaned Bertie, wiping his nose on his hand.

Mum sighed wearily. Bertie had trouble staying clean for five minutes, let alone a whole day.

"Tell you what," she said, "I'll make you a deal. If you bring home a nice class photo I'll take you to that water park."

"Splash City?" gasped Bertie.

Splash City had just opened in town and all Bertie's friends had been. It had a giant bubble pool, six flumes and the Rocky Rapids River Ride. Bertie was willing to do anything for a trip to Splash City – even stay clean for a day.

"Is it a deal?" said Mum.

"Deal," said Bertie, excitedly.

"Good. Have you got your hanky?"

Bertie pulled it out of his pocket.

"Remember to use it before the photo," said Mum. "I don't want a picture of you with a runny nose."

"OK!" sighed Bertie.

"And don't lose it. No hanky, no trip to Splash City – understand?"

Bertie tucked his hanky up his sleeve and hurried off down the road. He couldn't wait for the weekend. All he had to do was stay clean for one day – how hard could it be?

CHAPTER 2

Bertie stood in the playground with his friends, waiting for the bell.

"What's that funny smell?" asked Darren, holding his nose.

"It's Bertie," grinned Eugene. "He's had a bath!"

Darren sniffed Bertie. "Phew! You smell of flowers!"

"It's just shampoo!" said Bertie.

"And what's wrong with your hair?" said Eugene.

Bertie rolled his eyes. "My mum did it. It's for the photo."

"I think you look sweet," giggled Donna.

"SWEET?" hooted Darren. "He looks like an alien! Anyway, I bet you can't stay like that for five minutes."

"That's where you're wrong," said Bertie. "'Cos if I stay clean my mum's taking me to Splash City."

Just then a pale boy arrived carrying a briefcase. It was Bertie's arch-enemy, Know-All Nick. Nick halted and stared at Bertie. Bertie stared back. They looked like twins.

"What happened to you?" sneered Nick.

"Nothing," said Bertie.

"You look weird. Have you brushed your hair?"

Bertie sighed.

"If you must know it's for the photo. I thought I'd look smart."

"You? Smart? HA! HA!" scoffed Nick.

Bertie glanced down. Nick was standing close to a large brown puddle. If he jumped in it now he could splash Nick with muddy water. But he was bound to get dirty as well – and he'd promised his mum to stay clean. Still, there was always tomorrow.

He turned to go. "See you later, smarty-pants."

Dirty Bertie

Miss Boot prowled the front of the classroom.

"I trust you've all remembered that we're having our class photo today," she said. "And this year I don't want anyone spoiling it – Bertie."

"Me?" said Bertie.

"Yes, you," glared Miss Boot. "Don't think I've forgotten last year."

"That wasn't my dog!" said Bertie. "He followed me into school…"

"Quiet!" barked Miss Boot. "This year there will be no dogs and no silliness, do I make myself clear?"

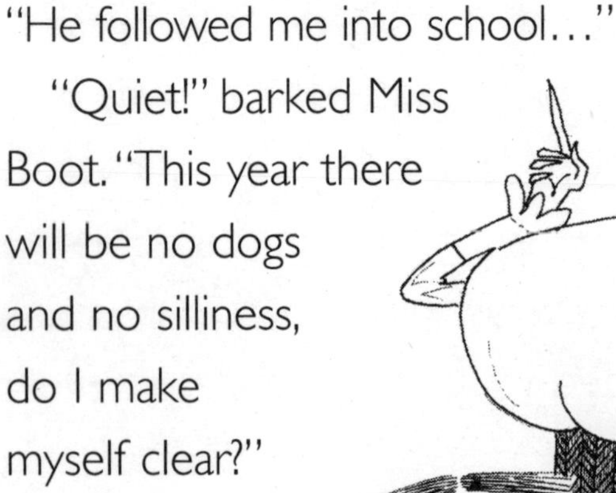

"Yes, Miss Boot," chorused the class.

"Good. The photographer is arriving at one o'clock, so we will gather in the hall after lunch."

Bertie groaned. After lunch? That meant he had to get through an entire morning without getting dirty. Still, it would be worth it. Bertie sniffed. He was about to wipe his nose on his sleeve when he remembered his hanky. He reached into his trouser pocket. He turned cold. It wasn't there! He checked his other pocket.

Empty!

What was it his mum had said? *No hanky, no trip to Splash City.* Bertie slumped forward on his desk. This was terrible – if he didn't find it, there'd be no Rocky Rapids River Ride.

Miss Boot was busy writing sums on the board. Slowly, Bertie slid down in his seat and disappeared under his desk. His eyes swept across the floor. No sign of a hanky. He began to crawl on all fours, weaving his way through a forest of legs. The floor was littered with sweet wrappers, stickers, chewing gum, rubbers, apple cores and dead bluebottles – but no hanky.

"OW!"

Uh oh – he'd accidentally crawled over someone's foot.

"Nicholas!" cried Miss Boot. "Get on with your work!"

"It wasn't me, Miss," whined Know-All Nick. "Someone kicked me!"

"Don't talk nonsense!" snapped Miss Boot.

Bertie kept very still. Suddenly Nick's head appeared under the desk and their eyes met. Bertie put a finger to his lips and shook his head. A sly smile spread across Nick's face.

"It's Bertie, Miss!" cried Nick. "He's under the table!"

Bertie groaned. Trust Know-All to tell tales.

"BERTIE!" thundered Miss Boot. "COME OUT FROM THERE, THIS MINUTE!"

Slowly Bertie crawled out and stood up. His trousers seemed to have got rather dusty. A lump of chewing gum was stuck to his knee.

"Well? What do you have to say for yourself?" demanded Miss Boot.

"Um … have you seen my hanky?" asked Bertie.

CHAPTER 3

Miss Boot kept Bertie in at morning break, which meant he had no chance to look for his missing hanky. By lunchtime he was beginning to panic. Time was running out. Maybe he'd dropped the hanky in the playground when he got to school?

Mr Grouch was over by the railings,

sweeping up litter. Normally Bertie did his best to avoid the caretaker. Mr Grouch didn't like children and he especially didn't like Bertie. Bertie was pretty sure that he turned into a vampire after dark. Nevertheless this was an emergency.

"Um … Mr Grouch?"

The caretaker carried on sweeping.

"I was wondering if you'd seen a hanky? It's sort of white..."

Mr Grouch scowled. "I know what a hanky looks like."

"Oh. Have you seen it?"

"Do I look like I'm running a lost property service?"

"No, but..."

Mr Grouch leaned heavily on his broom.

"Anything I find in this playground is treated as litter," he said. "Litter goes in the bin, got that?"

"Yes ... er, thanks," said Bertie, beating a hasty retreat.

Bertie hurried round the side of the school. He found two large, grey bins standing in a corner. They were taller than he was. Even standing on tiptoe he couldn't see inside.

Luckily help was at hand.

"Hi, Bertie. What are you doing?" asked Eugene, appearing at his side.

"Quick," said Bertie. "Get down."

"What?"

"I need to climb on your back!"

"But it's dirty!" grumbled Eugene. "I'm wearing my best clothes."

"This is an emergency," said Bertie. "I've got to find my hanky."

"What if Mr Grouch catches us?"

"He won't. Come on!"

Eugene sighed and got down on all fours. Bertie climbed on to his back. He lifted the lid of the first bin and peeped inside. It was full of leftovers from dinner. It smelled worse than one of Darren's burps.

"Can you see it?" asked Eugene.

"I'm looking. Keep still!" said Bertie.

"Hurry up, I can't hold you!"

Eugene was getting anxious. He thought he could hear footsteps. Someone was coming and he was sure it was Mr Grouch! He leaped to his feet.

"WOOOAHHHHH!" cried Bertie, losing his balance. He grabbed hold of the bin. It toppled towards him.

CRAAAASH!

Bertie surfaced from under a mountain of rotten cabbage and potato peel.

"S-sorry, Bertie!" stammered Eugene.

Bertie shook his head, scattering bits of vegetable in all directions.

"HEY YOU! COME HERE!" yelled an angry voice.

Mr Grouch was striding towards them waving his broom like a Roman spear.

Bertie didn't wait around to explain. He ran for his life.

Bertie ducked into the cloakroom to give Mr Grouch the slip. There were only five minutes till the end of lunch break and he still hadn't found his hanky.

"Phoo! What happened to you?" asked Know-All Nick, poking his head round the door. Bertie looked up. A white triangle peeped from Nick's top pocket. A hanky!

"Where did you get that?"

"This? It's mine," said Nick.

"Liar! You stole it! It's mine."

Bertie made a grab for it, but Nick dodged aside and waved the hanky under his nose.

"See, it's got the letter 'N' for Nicholas. I expect yours has a 'B' for Bogeynose."

Bertie glared at him.

"What's the matter?" taunted Nick. "Did poor lickle Bertie lose his hanky?"

"Get lost," Bertie snapped.

"Please yourself," shrugged Nick. "I was going to tell you where to find it, but maybe I won't."

"You've seen it?" said Bertie. "Where?"

Nick smiled slyly. "In the boys' toilets. But you'll have to hurry."

Bertie flew down the corridor. He raced past the classrooms, screeched round a corner and crashed through the door of the boys' toilets.

SPLOOSH! His feet went from under him and he sat down with a bump.

He looked around. The floor was ankle deep in water and his trousers were soaking wet. It was then that he noticed the sign on the door.

Bertie got soggily to his feet. That two-faced sneak had tricked him. There was no hanky. And now he was dripping wet *and* late for the class photo.

CHAPTER 4

Miss Boot arranged her class on the platform in the hall. At last everyone was in position. She counted the heads and groaned. Someone was missing and no prizes for guessing who.

Right on cue the door flew open and Bertie rushed in, panting for breath.

Miss Boot stared at him in horror.

"Good grief! What on earth have you been doing?"

"Me? Nothing," said Bertie.

"Look at the state of you!" said Miss Boot, clutching her head.

Bertie inspected himself. Come to think of it, he was a little messy. His trousers were caked in dust and dripping wet. His clean white shirt was stained a greenish brown. A wet puddle was spreading around his feet. He pushed back his hair and a piece of potato peel fell out.

"Go and get cleaned up," ordered Miss Boot. "No wait, there isn't time. Stand in the back row and try to keep out of sight."

Bertie splodged on to the platform and pushed his way to the back next to Darren.

The photographer bent over his camera.

"Everyone ready? Say cheese!"

"Cheese!" chorused the class.

"WAIT!" cried a voice.

Miss Boot groaned. "What is it *now*, Bertie?"

"I need to blow my nose."

"Then blow it. And use a hanky."

"That's the trouble," wailed Bertie. "I've been looking everywhere and I can't find it!"

"Then you'll *have to do without!*" screeched Miss Boot. "Now can we *please* get on with the photo?"

The photographer bent over his camera once more. Bertie's shoulders drooped. His nose was running but what did it matter? Once his mum discovered he'd lost his hanky there'd be no trip to Splash City.

He found a dry patch on his sleeve and wiped his nose. Wait a minute … what was that? A corner of white peeped out from under his cuff. And then he remembered. He'd stuffed his hanky into his sleeve that morning for safe keeping. He pulled it out triumphantly. Everything was going to be OK. He put the hanky to his nose and blew…

CLICK!

Mum was busy on the computer when she heard the front door open.

"Bertie, is that you? How did the photo go?"

"Fine," shouted Bertie, coming into the room.

Mum turned round. She turned pale. She looked like she might faint.

"Bertie...! WHAT HAVE YOU DONE?!" she gasped.

"It's OK!" beamed Bertie. "I lost my hanky but I found it. Look!"

He waved a soggy white rag.

"So," he said, "can we go?"

Mum stared. "Go? Go where?"

"To Splash City. You promised!"

Mum looked grim. "There's only one

place you're going, Bertie, and there won't be any splashing."

SPOOKY!

CHAPTER 1

Bertie couldn't wait – Darren and Eugene were coming for a sleepover and they were going to sleep in the tent in the garden. All he had to do was convince his parents.

"I'm sorry, Bertie," said Mum, "I don't think it's a good idea."

"Why not?" asked Bertie.

"Because last time you woke up all the neighbours!"

"We were only having a water fight."

"It was two in the morning! We had half the street banging on the door."

"We won't do it again," promised Bertie. "We'll be really, really quiet."

Mum sighed wearily. "In any case, I don't even know where the tent is."

Dad came into the kitchen.

"Dad," said Bertie, "do you know where the tent is?"

"Mmm? In the garage I expect."

"Can we sleep in it tonight?"

"I don't see why not."

"Great!" said Bertie.

The doorbell rang and he dashed off to answer it before his parents could change their minds.

"Guess what?" said Bertie, as Darren and Eugene staggered through the front door carrying their bags. "Mum and Dad said yes. We can sleep in the tent!"

"Brilliant!" said Darren. "We can have a water fight!"

They found the tent under a pile of junk at the back of the garage. It had been Dad's brilliant idea to buy it.

He said they'd have lots of wonderful family camping holidays and save a fortune. But as it turned out they'd only been camping once. It had rained all weekend, the tent nearly blew away in a gale and their sleeping bags had got soaked. They'd left in the morning with Mum vowing she would never go camping again.

Bertie shook out the contents of the bag on to the grass. Eugene stared at the jumble of pegs and poles.

"Shouldn't we read the instructions?" he asked.

"No need," said Bertie. "It's simple! I've done it hundreds of times!"

This wasn't strictly true – the tent had only been up twice and Bertie hadn't helped at all.

Bertie and Eugene wrestled with the poles while Whiffer got in the way and sat on the groundsheet. Darren lolled on the grass reading a comic.

At last they were finished and Bertie stood back to admire their work.

"It looks a bit wonky," frowned Darren.

"It's meant to be wonky," said Bertie.

"Can I let go of the pole now?" called Eugene from inside.

"Wait a minute!" answered Bertie. "I've got to do the pegs."

Bertie went round with a mallet hammering pegs into the ground. Darren went back to his comic. Whiffer was sniffing round the tent, eager to join in. He seized one of the guy ropes in his mouth and started to pull. The peg shot out. The tent leaned dangerously to one side.

"NO!" yelled Bertie. "Whiffer, let go!"

"GRRRR!" growled Whiffer, shaking his head from side to side.

"Bad dog!" cried Bertie, trying to grab the rope.

Whiffer backed away, the rope still in his teeth. The tent stretched. *And stretched.*

TWANG! A dozen pegs shot out of the ground and the tent collapsed in a heap.

"MNNNNFF HEEELP!" cried a voice from underneath.

"OK, Eugene, you can let go now," said Bertie.

CHAPTER 2

After supper, Dad went out to the garden to sort out the tent. Bertie sat in his bedroom with Darren and Eugene checking their supplies for the night.

"Comics?" said Bertie.

"Check."

"Torches?"

"Check."

"Midnight feast?"

"I brought the crisps," said Darren.

"I got the chocolate biscuits," said Bertie.

"I got some muesli bars," said Eugene.

The other two gave him a look.

"What? It's all I could get! My mum says they're good for you."

Bertie rolled his eyes. "What about weapons? Is everybody armed?"

Darren had a space gun he'd got for his birthday. Bertie tucked his pirate dagger into his belt. Only Eugene had forgotten.

"Why do we need weapons, anyway?" he asked.

Bertie shrugged. "Don't say we didn't warn you."

"It'll be dark," said Darren. "Really dark. You never know what might be *out there*."

Eugene turned pale. "You're just trying to scare me," he said.

Mum poked her head round the door.

"OK, the tent's all ready!"

"Great," said Bertie.

"Wicked!" said Darren.

"Hooray," gulped Eugene, gripping his torch.

Tiptoe, tiptoe, tiptoe. The three of them crept down the garden.

Bertie led the way with Eugene keeping close behind. In the dark the garden seemed much bigger than Bertie remembered. The moon was a ghostly white. The trees threw dancing shadows on the ground.

"Wait!" said Bertie, halting suddenly. "Where's Darren?"

They looked around. "He was here a minute ago," said Eugene.

They shone their torches into the bushes.

"Darren?" called Bertie. "Where are you?"

No answer. The tent flapped in the wind.

"Darren, this isn't funny. Come out!"

Silence.

"Maybe he went back for something?" whispered Eugene.

They looked back at the house. Whiffer watched them hopefully from the kitchen where he was locked in for the night.

There was a rustle in the bushes. Bertie swung round.

"Darren? Is that you?"

Deathly silence.

"Maybe we better wait in the tent," said Bertie.

"G-good idea," stammered Eugene.

They both bolted down the garden. Eugene wrestled with the zip…

"GRARRRRRRGH!"

Something burst out of the bushes and grabbed Bertie round the neck.

"YEEAARGH! HEEELP!" howled Bertie.

"HA! HA! HA!" giggled Darren. "Did I scare you?"

Bertie struggled free. "Course not."

"Liar! You practically wet your pants."

"Didn't."

"Did."

"Didn't. We knew it was you, didn't we, Eugene? *Eugene?*"

Eugene peeped his head out of the tent. "Has it gone?"

Darren was still going on about his clever trick as they got into their sleeping bags. *Right that's it*, thought Bertie. *Two can play at that game*. No one made a fool of Bertie, the terror of Class 3. Who had locked Mr Weakly in the cupboard? Who had turned the hose on Mr Grouch, the demon caretaker? *We'll soon find out which of us is the scaredy-cat*, scowled Bertie. By the time he had finished Darren would be begging for his mum.

CHAPTER 3

"Pass the crisps," said Bertie.

"All gone," said Darren.

"Throw me a biscuit, then."

"None left."

"There's still some muesli bars," said Eugene.

Bertie burped. Wrappers, crisp packets and biscuit crumbs littered the tent.

He brushed them off his sleeping bag. They'd read their comics, made shadows with their torches and eaten their midnight feast, but still none of them felt the least bit sleepy. The wind moaned outside.

"I've got an idea," said Bertie. "Let's tell *ghost stories*."

"No!" wailed Eugene.

"What's the matter? Scared you might have nightmares?" taunted Darren. "I love ghost stories, the scarier the better."

"Who's going first then?" asked Bertie.

"Eugene," said Darren.

"Why me?" moaned Eugene. "I don't know any ghost stories."

"Just make one up," said Bertie. "And to make it even spookier we'll turn off our torches."

Eugene turned pale. "But it'll be dark."

"Great," said Darren. "I love the dark."

"Me too," said Bertie. "Everyone ready?"

CLICK! Off went the torches. The tent was plunged into blackness.

Eugene cleared his throat. "Once upon a time there were three bears..."

Darren groaned. "That's not a ghost story!"

"It is, it's about ghosts."

"You said it was about three bears!"

"It is. They're ghost bears."

Eugene started again. "Once upon a time there were three ghost bears who lived in a little ghost cottage in the ghost wood..."

"This is rubbish!" grumbled Darren. "It's a fairy story!"

"No it isn't!"

"Yes it is! I bet Goldilocks comes and sits on the ghost chairs and eats the ghost porridge!"

"If you're so clever you tell a story," said Eugene sulkily.

Bertie saw his chance. "I've got one," he said. He was going to tell a story so hair-raising that Darren would be begging him to stop.

"It was a dark, dark night," Bertie began. "The wind was moaning."

"Wooo wooooo!" moaned Darren.

"Three boys were camping in a spooky haunted wood. Suddenly they heard—"

Bertie broke off.

"W-what? Suddenly they heard what?" asked Eugene.

"Shhh!" said Bertie. "Listen!"

"Don't!" whimpered Eugene. "You're scaring me."

"Oooh, me too!" said Darren, giggling.

Bertie shook his head. "I'm serious. I think I heard something."

"It's a ghost! We're all going to DIEEEEE!" wailed Darren, clutching his throat and falling back on his pillow.

"Shut up!" hissed Bertie. "Listen!"

They all held their breath and listened.

THUMP!

Help! thought Bertie. *There really is something out there.*

Footsteps came down the path. Closer and closer. Bertie froze. Darren gripped his arm. Suddenly the tent flap was unzipped and they were blinded by light.

"ARGHHHHHHH!" they yelled.

"What's going on?" Mum shone a torch in their faces. "I came to check if everyone was OK."

Bertie heaved a sigh of relief. "We're fine," he said. "We were just going to sleep."

"Yes," said Eugene. "Only first I need the toilet!"

CHAPTER 4

"Eugene?" whispered Bertie. "Eugene, are you awake?"

Eugene snored.

"Darren?"

Darren wheezed. Only Bertie couldn't sleep. How long had he been lying awake? Hours and hours. It must be the middle of the night. The ground was hard, his feet were like blocks of ice and a howling draught was coming from somewhere. Worst of all, he kept thinking he could hear noises outside. Strange, scuffling, moving-about noises.

"Mum?" called Bertie, anxiously. "Mum, is that you?"

No answer. His parents would be fast asleep by now. They wouldn't hear him, even if he screamed. Of course he was only imagining things. It was the wind in the trees. Or the tent creaking. It couldn't be anything else – like a headless ghost for instance. Ghosts were only in ghost stories. If he peeped outside there was no chance at all he'd see a ghost. But just in case, maybe it was safer to stay in the tent. Nothing could get at him in here ... unless it came through the walls.

THUD!

Bertie sat bolt upright. He had *definitely* heard something that time. He switched on his torch. How he wished he was back in his own bed. Whose stupid idea was it to sleep outside in a tent? Didn't his parents care if he was eaten alive?

SCUFFLE, SCUFFLE, SCUFFLE.

"HELLO?" croaked Bertie.

No answer. If he was going to come face to face with a headless ghost, he didn't want to do it alone.

"Darren!" he hissed.

Darren went on snoring.

"Darren, wake up!"

"Urhhhh? Whasssgoingon?"

"Listen!" said Bertie. "Something's out there!"

Darren yawned and rolled over. "Yeah, yeah. Nice try, Bertie."

"No, I'm not joking this time! There is!"

Darren raised his head an inch.

SCRATCH, SCRATCH, SCRATCH.

He gasped. He reached under his pillow for his space gun. Bertie gripped his pirate dagger and put a finger to his lips. Maybe if they were quiet as mice the ghost would pass on by?

THUMP!

Arghhh! It was right outside the tent. Bertie could hear its heavy breathing. He froze in horror. The door of the tent was gaping open! Eugene must have forgotten to zip it up when he'd come back from the toilet. No wonder the tent was as cold as the grave!

Bertie pointed. "Close ... the ... zip!"

"You close it!" squeaked Darren.

The thing was scratching at the tent, trying to get in. Bertie pointed the beam of his torch. Help!

A gigantic shadow with savage teeth and a monstrous head loomed on the side of the tent.

The next moment the thing burst in and was on top of him.

"GET IT OFF! IT'S EATING ME!" screamed Bertie.

"HA! HA! HA!" Darren was doubled up with laughter.

Bertie sat up, pushing the monster off him. He stared at his floppy-eared attacker, who was now crunching on a muesli bar.

"WHIFFER! How did he get out?"

Darren grinned. "Someone must have forgotten to close the back door."

"Eugene!" said Bertie. "I'll kill him. Wait a moment. Where is he?"

They both shone their torches. From the corner of the tent came the sound of peaceful snoring.

Mum unzipped the flap, flooding the tent with morning light.

"Good morning!" she said, brightly. "How did you all sleep?"

"Great, thanks!" Eugene sat up and stretched.

In his sleeping bag, Bertie groaned. All night long he'd had Whiffer lying on top of him, tossing and turning and whining in his sleep. Eugene and Darren had taken it in turns to snore the loudest. Bertie hadn't slept a wink.

"Who's for breakfast?" asked Mum. "Bacon and eggs?"

Bertie turned a shade of green. He wriggled out of his sleeping bag and crawled out of the tent.

"Bertie?" said Mum. "Where are you going?"

"Back to bed!" groaned Bertie.

Dirty Bertie

GERMS!

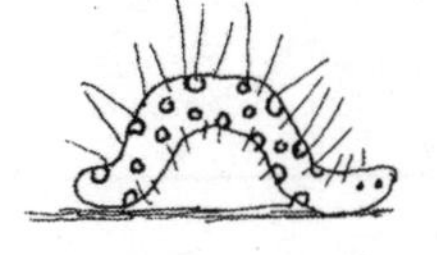

For Sam, who I'm sure would love
"The Dead Skunks" ~ D R
For Ella – Bertie's no. 1 fan ~ A M

Contents

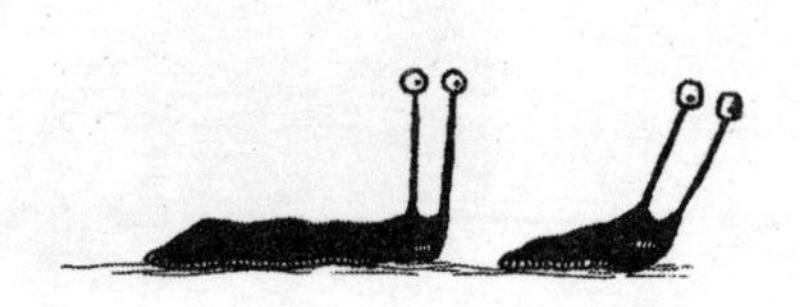

GERMS!

CHAPTER 1

"Are you all right?" said Mum. "You don't look well."

Bertie looked up from his breakfast. His mum was talking to Suzy, who had just drooped into the kitchen.

"I'm hot," she moaned.

"Actually I'm a bit hot," said Bertie, through a mouthful of cereal.

"My head aches," croaked Suzy. "I ache all over."

"My head's sort of achey," said Bertie. "It aches when I talk."

Mum paid no attention. "Let me look at you," she said to Suzy. "Goodness! Look at these spots! I think you've got chickenpox."

"Chickenpox?" groaned Suzy.

"Chickenpox!" said Bertie.

Mum fetched her big blue medical book and turned the pages. "Here it is," she said. "Chickenpox: small itchy red spots, fever, and aches and pains. Yes, you've definitely got it. No school for a week, I'm afraid."

"A WEEK?" said Bertie.

Suzy stuck out her tongue and drooped back upstairs to bed.

"What about me?" asked Bertie, pulling up his shirt. "My tummy's a bit blotchy. Do you think that's chickenpox?"

"I think that's dirt," said Mum. "Now finish your breakfast. And keep away from Suzy, chickenpox is very catching."

Bertie sighed. It wasn't fair. How come his sister caught chickenpox when he never got anything? If anyone ought to catch something it was him. He hardly *ever* washed his hands. Now Suzy would get a whole week off school while he had to sit through boring lessons with Miss Boot. Bertie gulped. He'd just remembered what day it was. Friday – homework day. As usual Bertie had put off doing his homework until the last minute. Then at the last minute he'd forgotten altogether. Miss Boot, however, would not forget. Anyone who didn't hand in their homework on time risked execution or worse.

If only I had chickenpox, thought Bertie. He felt his head. It did feel a bit hot. He scratched under his arm. He was definitely a bit itchy. The more he thought about it the more he was convinced he was getting it.

"MU-UM!" he wailed. "I don't feel well!"

"There's nothing wrong with you," said Mum. "You just ate two bowls of cereal."

"Yes, but that was before. Now I feel sick!"

"Don't talk nonsense, Bertie. Hurry up and clean your teeth."

Bertie stomped upstairs to the bathroom. How come no one ever believed him? For all they knew he could be dying! He looked in the mirror. *Just my luck*, he thought. *Not a single spot.*

But wait a minute, didn't Mum say chickenpox was catching? Well then he'd just have to catch it. After all, why should his greedy sister keep it all to herself?

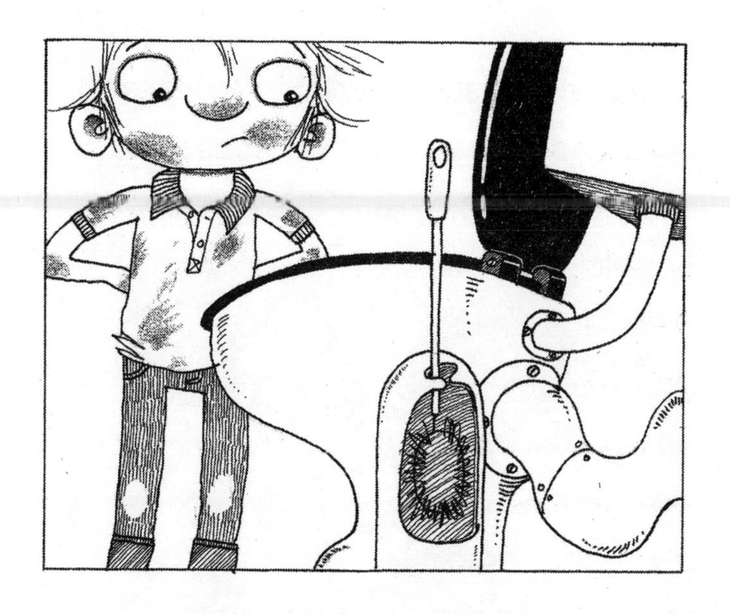

CHAPTER 2

Germs, thought Bertie. That's what he needed. Germs spread diseases – and luckily they were everywhere. His parents were always saying, "Don't touch that, Bertie, it's covered in germs!" Cats and dogs had germs. Toilets were crawling with them. You got germs from picking your nose or eating sweets off the floor.

Bertie had always wanted to examine some germs under a microscope. He imagined tiny armies of them, with scowling faces and hairy legs. Cold germs would be green. Chicken-pox germs would be spotty. But where did you catch them? Bertie looked around and his eye fell on Suzy's pink toothbrush. That would be covered in her germs! He squeezed out a large blob of toothpaste. Cleaning your teeth with your sister's toothbrush was a bit disgusting, even for him, but if it meant missing school it would be worth it.

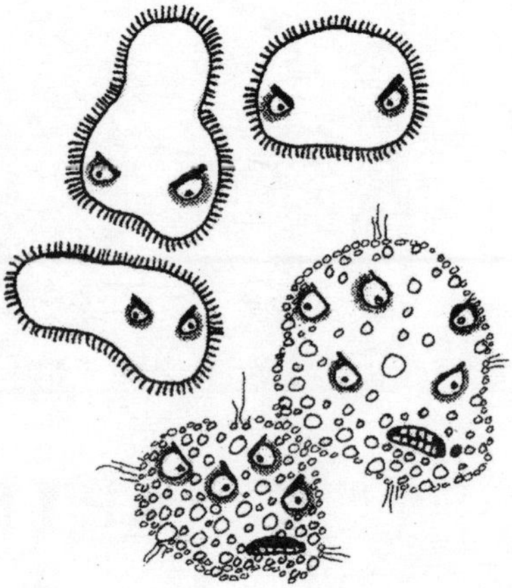

"Bertie!" called Mum. "What are you doing up there?"

"Nothing!" shouted Bertie. "Just cleaning my teeth."

He swallowed some toothpaste to give the germs a better chance to work. Then he stared at his face in the mirror and waited. Unbelievable – not a single spot! What did you have to do to catch a few measly germs?

On the landing he met Mum carrying a glass of lemonade.

"Is that for Suzy?" asked Bertie. "Can I take it to her?"

"Why?" said Mum, suspiciously.

"I'm just being helpful."

"Hmm," said Mum. "Better not, I don't want you catching her germs."

"I won't!" said Bertie. "I won't even go near her. I'll just put it down where she can reach it."

Mum eyed Bertie strangely. It wasn't like him to offer to help. "OK, but don't spill any. And don't go bothering her!"

Bertie smiled to himself. Once Suzy had drunk from the glass it would be covered in her germs. One little sip of that lemonade and he'd be drinking billions of them.

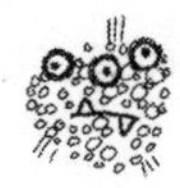  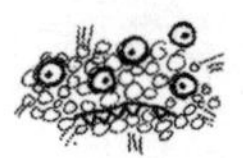

Suzy was sitting up in bed, looking pale.

"What do you want?" she groaned.

"I brought you some lemonade," said Bertie, smiling sweetly.

Suzy narrowed her eyes. "Why? What are you up to?"

"Nothing," said Bertie. "I'm just looking after you."

"You don't fool me," said Suzy.

"You want to catch my chickenpox so you can stay off school."

"I don't!" lied Bertie. "Have some lemonade!"

"I'm not thirsty."

"Just a sip."

"Go away!"

"Let me help," said Bertie, pressing the glass to Suzy's lips. He tipped it up. Suzy choked and spluttered. Lemonade spilled on her pyjamas and splashed the sheets.

"MUUUM!" wailed Suzy. "BERTIE'S BEING MEAN!"

Mum's feet pounded up the stairs.

"What's going on?" she demanded.

"Nothing!" cried Bertie.

"BERTIE WET THE BED!" howled Suzy.

"Bertie!" shouted Mum. "GET OUT!"

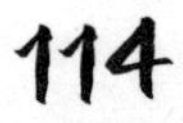

Bertie escaped to his bedroom. He still had the glass and luckily there was a little lemonade left in the bottom. He could almost see the germs swimming around like tiny tadpoles. *Chickenpox here I come!* he thought, gulping down the drink in one go. He ran to the bathroom and stared at his face. A minute passed. Two minutes. He inspected his belly. Not a single spot or blotch. *This is so unfair,* thought Bertie. Suzy got chickenpox without even trying!

Time was running out. Any minute now Mum would drag him off to school and he would have to face Miss Boot. There was no escape. Unless … he suddenly remembered his mum's big blue medical book. Bertie found it on the kitchen table. Boils, bruises, burns … chickenpox – here it was!

Bertie read it twice through then closed the book. *Maybe I don't actually need to catch anything*, he thought. He just had to make Mum *believe* he had chickenpox. Then he'd be safe. No Miss Boot, no school and no handing in smelly homework.

CHAPTER 3

"Bertie, where are you? We need to go!" yelled Mum.

Bertie dragged himself downstairs and slumped into the hall.

"I'm tired," he moaned.

"Don't droop," said Mum. "We're late and I need to get back to Suzy. Now hurry up."

She opened the front door and marched off down the road.

Bertie dawdled behind at a snail's pace.

"Can't you walk a bit faster?" grumbled Mum.

"I'm tired!" moaned Bertie. "My legs hurt!"

"Bertie, stop all this nonsense!" said Mum. "There's nothing wrong with you! Now get a move on!"

"There is!" wailed Bertie. "I've got aches and pains."

"Where?"

"All over," said Bertie.

Mum rolled her eyes. "I don't have time for this, Bertie. You're going to school and that's that."

She strode off down the road. Bertie made I'm-going-to-be-sick noises.

Mum kept walking.

"Blech! Urggle!" Bertie sounded as if he was choking.

Mum spun round. "NOW WHAT?"

"I think I'm going to be sick!"

"So which is it then? Your legs hurt or you're feeling sick?"

"Both," said Bertie. "I think I must be really catching it."

"Catching what?"

"Chickenpox!"

Mum bent down to examine his face. "Chickenpox, eh?" she said. "So where are the spots then? Show me."

Whoops, thought Bertie. He'd completely forgotten about the spots.

Mum folded her arms. "Oh dear, yes, this is serious," she said. "Very serious. I see what you've got. It's *homework-itus*."

"Um, is that bad?" asked Bertie.

"Very bad. You catch it when you don't do your homework. There's only one cure, I'm afraid."

"Staying at home?" asked Bertie, hopefully.

"No," said Mum. "Telling your teacher. I'm sure Miss Boot will know what to do. Come on!"

CHAPTER 4

They reached the school gates. Bertie waved to his friends Darren and Eugene, who were clutching their homework books, ready to hand in. Miss Boot was prowling the playground glaring at anyone who dared to make a noise. Over by the railings Bertie spotted Angela Nicely, sucking on a stick of liquorice.

Angela lived next door to Bertie. She was six years old and madly in love with him. Normally he tried to avoid her, but right now she was his only chance.

"Is that liquorice?" asked Bertie.

"Yes," beamed Angela, proudly. "I bought it with my pocket money."

"Can I have a bit?"

Angela shook her head. "No! It's mine!"

"Go on, just a little bit."

"I already sucked it. It's got my germs!" said Angela, waving the soggy liquorice.

"I'll swap you my apple," said Bertie.

"No thanks."

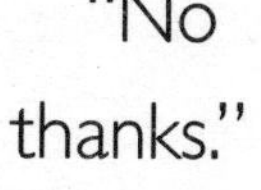

Bertie didn't have much time. His Mum had finished chatting to Mrs Nicely and was getting ready to go.

"I'll give you fifty pence," he said. "I'll bring it to school on Monday."

Angela considered. She could buy a lot of liquorice with fifty pence.

"Brownie's honour?" she said.

"Yes, yes, Brownie's honour."

Angela took a last suck of the liquorice and handed it over. Bertie popped it swiftly in his mouth and chewed. Mum was coming. "Bye, then, Bertie. Have a good day at school."

Bertie swallowed. "Mmmmnhh!" he groaned.

"What?"

Bertie pointed to his throat. "Mmmmnh! Mmmmnh!" he croaked.

"What? I can't hear what you're saying!"

"My throat hurts!"

Mum sighed heavily. "Bertie, we've been through all this. There's nothing wrong with you."

"There is!"

"OK, show me. Open your mouth."

Bertie opened his mouth and stuck out his tongue.

"GOOD HEAVENS!" shrieked Mum. "IT'S BLACK! WHY DIDN'T YOU SAY SO BEFORE?"

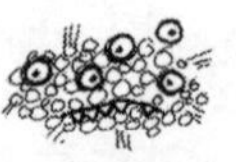

Bertie lay on the sofa and zapped on the TV. It was going to be a brilliant day. Suzy felt too sick to leave her bed so he had the front room all to himself. He gulped down some lemonade and slurped up another spoonful of chocolate ice cream. It had all worked out perfectly. Mum had wanted to call

the doctor straight away, but by the time they got home his tongue was looking much better. Still, she decided it was best to keep him off school. Bertie smiled to himself as he took another swig of lemonade. He didn't have to face Miss Boot and he hadn't even had to catch any horrible spots.

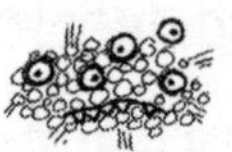

Next morning, Bertie woke up early. *Brilliant*, he thought. *Saturday!* Thc sun was shining and he didn't have to go to school. He threw on his clothes and dashed downstairs.

"Oh, you're up," said Mum. "How are you feeling this morning?"

"Much better," said Bertie. "Can I go to the park with Darren and Eugene?"

"Certainly not," said Mum. "I don't want them catching your germs."

Bertie frowned. "I haven't got any germs," he said. "I'm better now. I thought I was catching something, but it turns out I wasn't."

"Really?" said Mum. "Have you looked in the mirror?"

Bertie felt his face. Suddenly he felt itchy. And hot. He dashed into the hall and stared at his reflection in the mirror.

It couldn't be! It was! His face was covered in hundreds of spots!

STOMP!

CHAPTER 1

Bertie loved Sunday afternoons. Gran often dropped in for tea and brought one of her yummy home-made cakes. Today it was Bertie's favourite: Triple Chocolate Fudge Cake.

"Bertie," said Gran. "What are you doing next Saturday?"

"Nuffink," replied Bertie with his

mouth full.

"Well how would you like to go dancing with me?"

Bertie choked, spraying cake crumbs all over the table.

"ME?"

"Yes, I'm entering a competition and I'm stuck for a partner. Stan's put his back out mowing the lawn."

"But I can't dance!" said Bertie.

"Of course you can. You've got two feet."

"And you went to the school disco," Mum pointed out.

"I didn't dance!" said Bertie, horrified. "I just ate crisps!"

"Well, I'm sure you'd get the hang of it with a little practice. Please, Bertie. For your gran."

Bertie shook his head. No way was he going anywhere near a dance floor … especially not with Gran. The kind of dancing she did was the kind he'd seen on telly. *Ballroom dancing!* It was all prancing round in tight trousers and fluffy petticoats. There was no way Gran was going to talk him into this one! He'd rather eat dog food than have to dance like that.

Gran sighed. "Oh well, I'll just have to find someone else to share the prize."

Bertie paused mid-mouthful. "What prize?"

"No never mind, if you're not interested."

"I am! What prize?"

"Well, if we won the contest, the prize is a luxury cruise to New York."

Bertie's eyes boggled. New York! Land of hot dogs and hamburgers! A luxury cruise meant a swimming pool and his own servants. Maybe the captain would even let him steer the boat into New York!

"And would I have to take time off school?" he asked.

"Well if you won, I suppose so," said Mum.

"I'll do it!" declared Bertie.

"YEEE HOOOOO!" yelled Gran, grabbing him by the hands. She whirled him round and round the kitchen, until she got dizzy and collapsed into a chair.

Yikes! thought Bertie. *If this is what she calls dancing, we're in trouble!*

CHAPTER 2

The following evening, Gran dragged Bertie along to her dance class. He stared in horror at the couples shuffling round the hall. Most of them looked older than Egyptian mummies.

Miss Twist, the teacher, stepped forward. She was tall and thin as a ruler, with her hair scraped back into a bun.

"How lovely to see a new member," she trilled. "A special welcome to Bertie!"

The class clapped. Bertie doubted that they'd be clapping once they saw him dance.

Miss Twist divided them into groups to practise their steps. They began with the waltz.

"And step ... step ... slide-together," chanted Miss Twist. "Bertie, glide, not stamp! And stop looking at your feet!"

Bertie groaned. This was impossible. How could he tell what his feet were doing if he couldn't look at them?

"One, two, three. One, two, three," went the class, gliding like swans.

CLUMP! STOMP! STOMP!

CLUMP! STOMP! STOMP! went Bertie, clomping like an elephant.

Things got worse when it was time to dance with Gran. She was twice as tall as Bertie, so he found himself squashed against her chest.

Gran sighed. "You're meant to be leading!"

"How can I lead if I can't see where I'm going?" moaned Bertie.

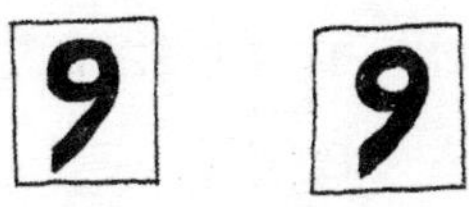

At last it was time for a break.

"Phew, I'm pooped!" wheezed Gran, mopping her brow. Bertie bought a can of drink and sat down beside her.

They watched a tall, sun-tanned couple practising their steps. The man had hair like Elvis. They whirled across the floor as if they were glued together.

"Good, aren't they?" said Bertie.

Gran rolled her eyes. "That's Keith and Kerry-Anne – South East Champions, as they never fail to mention. They're hot favourites to win on Saturday."

Bertie gaped. "You mean we've got to beat *them*?"

"I'm afraid so."

Keith was stamping and waving his arms as if he was trying to take off.

"What's he doing?" asked Bertie.

"It's called the *paso doble*," Gran explained. "It's like a bullfight."

Bertie's eyes lit up. A bullfight? Now that was *his* kind of dancing. Much better than a drippy old waltz. Bertie imagined he was a famous matador entering the bullring. He swept off his red cape and bowed. The crowd chanted his name: "EL BERTO! EL BERTO! EL..."

"BERTIE!" hissed Gran, prodding him in the ribs.

Bertie looked up to see the South East Champions beaming down at him. Close up, Keith's hair looked like a racoon's bottom.

He patted Bertie on the head. "Hello, little man. Having a good time?"

"I was," scowled Bertie.

Kerry-Anne laid a hand on Gran's arm. "Oh Dotty, so *sorry* to hear about poor old Stan. So you won't have a partner for Saturday! *Isn't* that a shame, Keith?"

Keith yawned. "Yeah, shame. Still, you were never likely to win, were you?"

"Oh, don't worry," said Gran. "I'm not giving up. I've found a new partner, haven't I, Bertie?"

Bertie opened his mouth and let out a burp. Keith and Kerry-Anne burst out laughing.

"HA! HA! Oh that's so SWEET! Your grandson! HA HA!"

Gran folded her arms. "I don't see what's so funny. Bertie happens to be a very talented dancer."

"Yes," said Bertie. "And I've watched it on TV."

"Then you probably know we're the South East Champions – three years running," boasted Keith. "Our *paso doble* is legendary!"

"Huh!" said Bertie. "We're doing the passo doobie, aren't we, Gran?"

Gran's eyebrows nearly hit the ceiling.

"You?" scoffed Keith. "You couldn't dance the hokey-cokey! Come on, Kerry-Anne, let's leave these amateurs to their dreams."

Bertie nudged Gran. "Did you see that? He's wearing a *wig*!"

"Never mind that," groaned Gran. "Why did you tell them we're going to dance the *paso doble*?"

Bertie shrugged. "It just came out. Anyway, I thought you wanted to win?"

"I do. But the *paso doble* takes months of practice!"

Bertie slurped the rest of his drink. "Well then, we better get started."

CHAPTER 3

For the rest of the week Bertie practised every spare minute. He was determined that he and Gran were going to win the contest. No way were creepy Keith and Kerry-Anne winning that luxury cruise.

Bertie threw himself into learning to dance like a matador. He practised his steps in his bedroom, stomping up and down until his dad yelled at him to be quiet. He practised on his way to school – which drew funny looks from people at the bus stop. And on Friday Mum found him having a tug-of-war with Whiffer in the kitchen.

"Bertie! What on earth are you doing?" she cried.

"Practising!" panted Bertie.

Mum took a closer look. "That's not my best scarf, is it?"

"I've only borrowed it. I need it for my costume."

"It's filthy! Take it out of Whiffer's mouth!"

"I'm trying!" gasped Bertie. "He won't … let … go!"

There was the sound of something ripping. Whiffer let go.

"Phew!" puffed Bertie, sitting down. "Dancing is hard work."

Saturday, the day of the contest, arrived. The finals were at the Regency Ballroom. Bertie's family were coming even though he'd begged them to stay away. Suzy said she wouldn't miss it for the world.

On the way Gran and Bertie called in at the hire shop to pick up their costumes. Gran's dress was Spanish, with bright red polka dots. Unfortunately, it was made for someone a lot smaller than her. Bertie stood outside the changing rooms while she wrestled with the zip.

"You'll have to breathe in," panted the shop assistant.

"I AM breathing in!" moaned Gran.

Bertie had a smart matador's costume with a black hat and a scarlet cape. He stood in front of a tall mirror, swirling the cape like a bullfighter.

"Olé! Olé! Ol-oops!" A stack of boxes toppled off the counter. Quickly he bent down to pick them up. The boxes contained practical jokes such as ice-cube flies and whoopee cushions. Most interesting of all was a small red box.

Bertie's eyes gleamed. Think what you could do with itching powder! You could use it on someone you didn't like – Keith or Kerry-Anne for instance. Come to think of it, that wasn't a bad idea. It might even help him to win the contest.
He slipped the box into his pocket and left some money on the counter.

CHAPTER 4

At the Regency Ballroom the audience were taking their seats. Bertie and Gran hurried backstage to get ready. While Gran pinned up her hair in front of the mirror, Bertie looked around … now was his chance.

He set off in search of their rivals. He found Kerry-Anne in her private dressing room, wearing a petticoat and a scowl.

"What do you think you're doing?" she snapped.

"Oh, sorry, I was um … looking for Gran," said Bertie.

"She's not here," said Kerry-Anne. "But since you've barged in, you can make yourself useful. Fetch me my dress from the rail. It's the blue one with the sequins."

Bertie closed the door. This was too good a chance to miss. He found the dress on the rail. Checking to see no one was watching, he took out the red box from his pocket.

Keith's laugh boomed from the next room. "HA HA! It's hilarious! The kid hardly comes up to her waist!"

That did it. Bertie shook some of the orange powder into the lining of the dress. It wouldn't take long to work – then they would see who was hilarious.

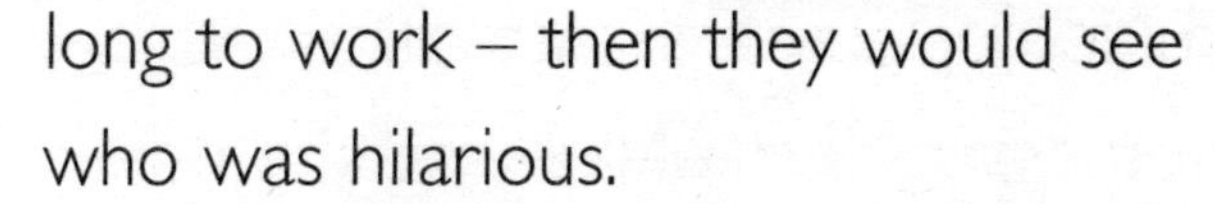

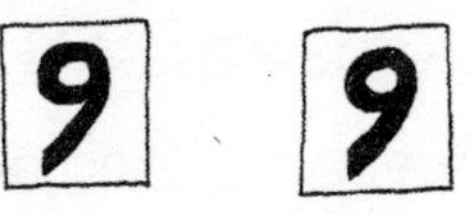

"Ladies and Gentlemen, will our dancers please take to the floor for the *paso doble*!"

The lights dimmed and a trumpet fanfare split the air. *This is it*, thought Bertie.

His costume was making him sweat. Worse still, his cape was so long it kept getting under his feet.

"Bertie, we're on!" whispered Gran, shoving him in the back. Bertie stumbled on to the floor. The audience giggled. They'd never seen a matador wearing plimsolls. Gran skidded into the spotlight, grabbing Bertie to keep her balance.

In the front row, Mum, Dad and Suzy tried to keep a straight face. The music started. Keith, Kerry-Anne and the other couples wove patterns across the floor.

Bertie swirled his red cape round and round. He was El Berto the fearless matador.

STOMP! STOMP! went his feet.

SWISH! SWISH! went his cape.

STOMP!

SWISH! ... ARGH! The cape had gone right over his head.

Bertie blundered about blindly, trying to get it off.

"Ow!" He collided with something soft. It was Gran and the two of them wobbled and swayed like wrestlers on ice. Gran stepped on the train of her dress and fell over. Bertie landed on top of her.

"LOOK OUT!" cried one of the couples, but it was too late…

CRAAAAAASH!

THUMP!

THUD!

Bertie pulled off the hat which had fallen over his eyes. Dancers lay struggling in a messy heap of arms, legs, bows and ruffles. Bertie clambered off Gran, whose dress had split at the back revealing her winter vest.

A judge was marching towards them with a clipboard and a grim expression. Bertie had a feeling his dancing days were over.

3 1 0

Gran and Bertie sat watching the final in progress. The judges had disqualified them as a danger to other contestants.

"Oh well," said Gran. "We did our best. Sorry we won't be going to New York."

"It's OK," shrugged Bertie.

"It's just a pity those two show-offs are going to win," said Gran. "They'll be bragging for weeks. Look at them!"

Bertie watched Keith lift Kerry-Anne over his head. Her shoulders twitched.

"I wouldn't be so sure," he said. "Maybe things are just warming up."

Certainly Kerry-Anne was beginning to act rather strangely. She was wriggling around as if she had ants in her pants.

Down on the dance floor, the itching powder was beginning to work.

"What's wrong with you?" hissed Keith.

"I can't help it!" she moaned. "It's this dress. It's so itchy!"

She clawed at her back.

"Stop doing that!" snapped Keith. "People are staring! Pull yourself together!"

"I'm trying!" squealed Kerry-Anne. "But… Eeek! Argh! Ohh! It itches!"

She stamped her feet and pawed at her arms. She scratched her back like a dog with fleas. Keith tried to grab her hands, but she shook him off.

"DON'T JUST STAND THERE!" she yelled. "DO SOMETHING! I'M ON FIRE!"

Keith did what you do when something is on fire. He snatched a jug of water from the nearest table and emptied it over his partner's head.

There was a brief, terrible silence. Then Kerry-Anne screamed.

"ARGHHH! YOU … YOU … IDIOT!"

She swiped at Keith. He gasped and turned bright pink. Clutching at his bald head he fled from the hall.

"See!" shouted Bertie. "I told you it was a wig!"

The audience cheered. If this was ballroom dancing they wanted more.

Gran took off her glasses and wiped her eyes. "Well," she grinned. "That was the best show I've seen in years. I wonder what got into Kerry-Anne?"

Bertie looked blank. "Search me," he said. "Maybe she just had an itch."

Things hadn't worked out so badly in the end. He wouldn't be going to New York, but at least he still had the itching powder. And there was plenty left in the box.

I wonder if Miss Boot can dance? thought Bertie. There was one way to find out.

ZOMBIE!

CHAPTER 1

Mum put down the phone. "That was Gran. She can't come."

"What?" said Dad. "But she's babysitting tonight!"

"She was. But she went to the dentist today and now she's got toothache."

Dad groaned. "What are we going to do? Paul and Penny are expecting us."

Bertie looked up from the comic he was reading. "It's OK," he said. "I can look after myself."

It would be great not having a babysitter. Suzy was sleeping over at Bella's so he would have the house all to himself. He could have a perfect evening: scoffing crisps, watching TV, scoffing chocolate and staying up late. Gran was a hopeless babysitter anyway – she always fell asleep in the middle of playing pirates. And, besides, Bertie didn't see why he needed a babysitter. He wasn't a baby. He knew where the snacks were and how to work the TV, so he could look after himself.

Mum didn't agree.

"Don't be ridiculous, Bertie," she said. "We can't possibly leave you on your own."

"Why not?" asked Bertie.

"What if something happened?"

"Like what?"

"Like you burning down the house," said Dad.

Mum sighed. "I'll just have to ring Penny and cancel."

"We let them down last time," said Dad. "There must be *someone* who could babysit. What about Alice?"

"She's back at college."

"Jackie then?"

"She won't come, not after Bertie put a slug in her hair."

"It wasn't a slug!" protested Bertie. "It was a snail!"

"I know!" said Mum. "What about Kevin?"

Bertie looked up. Kevin? Spotty Kevin from over the road? Were they *mad*? He hardly ever spoke! Bertie thought he'd rather do his homework than spend an evening with Kevin!

"Does Kevin babysit?" asked Dad, doubtfully.

"It's worth a try. I'll ring his mum and find out."

Five minutes later it was all settled. "He's on his way," announced Mum.

"Oh don't worry about me!" said Bertie, bitterly. "You just go out and leave me with Frankenstein. I'm sure I'll be fine."

"Bertie, he's just a normal teenager," said Mum. "I expect he's a bit shy!"

"He doesn't look shy to me," said Bertie darkly. "He looks like a murderer."

"Anyway it'll be nice having a boy to babysit for a change," said Mum. "Maybe he likes playing games?"

Bertie scowled. He hated having babysitters. And Kevin was going to be the worst ever.

CHAPTER 2

DING DONG!

Mum hurried to open the door.

"Kevin! How are you?" she trilled. "Bertie's in the lounge. He's so excited you're babysitting!"

Kevin drooped into the lounge. He looked like he was going to a funeral. He was wearing black jeans, a black

T-shirt and a long black coat. His T-shirt said "The Dead Skunks" and had a picture of a skull on it. He stared at Bertie through a dark curtain of hair.

"Right, we better be off," said Mum, brightly. "Don't stay up late, Bertie."

"And don't make a mess," added Dad.

They hurried out, slamming the door behind them.

Kevin flopped into a chair. A heavy silence filled the room. Bertie picked his nose. He waited for Kevin to tell him to stop. Kevin just sat there like a dark cloud. Bertie looked at the ceiling and let out a loud burp. He glanced at Kevin. Kevin looked bored to death. Bertie plonked his feet on the coffee table. Kevin scratched one of his spots and examined his finger.

Bertie couldn't understand it. Most babysitters told him off in the first five minutes.

He looked around for something to do next. "I'm hungry," he announced.

Kevin looked at him.

"Usually Mum lets me have a snack when she goes out. Can I get one?"

Kevin shrugged. "Whatever."

Great! thought Bertie. Normally he had to go on and on for hours before he got a snack – and even then it was one measly biscuit. When Alice babysat she made him eat fruit. But Kevin didn't seem to care what he did.

Bertie stole into the kitchen. He eyed the "Treats" cupboard where Mum kept all the forbidden goodies. He wasn't allowed to snoop in there. Not since the time he'd made himself sick eating a family-size bar of chocolate. Still, one tiny little snack wouldn't hurt, and Mum would never find out. Bertie opened the cupboard and peeped inside.

A door creaked.

Bertie jumped, banging his head and dropping the bag of crisps he was holding. When he looked round Kevin was leaning in the doorway watching him. It was creepy how he could appear without making a sound.

"Oh, hi," said Bertie. "I was just um … getting some crisps."

"Yeah?" said Kevin.

"Do you want some? Crisps?"

Kevin shrugged. "If you want."

"Right. What flavour?" asked Bertie. "We've got plain, prawn cocktail or cheese and onion?"

Kevin took all three.

CRUNCH! CRUNCH! CHOMP!

Bertie watched in amazement as Kevin wolfed down the crisps. He chewed with his mouth open. He slurped and burped and dropped bits on the carpet. *And Mum and Dad say I'm a messy eater!* thought Bertie. They'd obviously never seen Kevin.

"Had enough?" asked Bertie.

Kevin dropped the empty bags on the floor.

"We've got biscuits."

"Yeah?" said Kevin.

"In the tin. Or chocolate bars – but Mum notices if they're missing."

"Yeah?"

"Yeah." Bertie thought it over. "I suppose one would be OK," he said.

CHAPTER 3

BUUUUURP!

Bertie lay back on the sofa and patted his full stomach. To tell the truth he felt a bit sick. Kevin wiped chocolate from around his mouth. The room was littered with crisp packets, chocolate bar wrappers and biscuit crumbs. Kevin glanced at the clock.

Uh oh, thought Bertie. It was almost nine o'clock – way past his bedtime.

"Mum usually lets me stay up late on Saturdays," said Bertie.

"Yeah?"

"Yeah, when I've got a babysitter."

Kevin shrugged. "Whatever."

Bertie could hardly believe his luck. He never got to stay up later than nine o'clock – even on Christmas Eve. Maybe if he could keep Kevin occupied he could stay up all night?

"Do you want to play a game?" he asked.

Kevin scratched a spot on his chin. Bertie wondered if he could see anything through all that hair.

"I don't mean a board game," said Bertie. "We could play pirate ships.

Or alien invasion. Or maybe have a pillow fight?"

Kevin stopped scratching.

WHACK! THUMP!

Bertie whacked Kevin. Kevin thwacked him back.

They bounced up and down walloping each other with pillows. *This is fantastic*, thought Bertie. Mum never let him have pillow fights or bounce on the sofa. She said something would get broken.

WHUMP!

Bertie swung his pillow back, knocking over a lamp. The lamp landed on a vase of flowers. It wobbled and fell over with a crash.

"Whoops!" said Bertie.

Dirty Bertie

WHUMP! Kevin's pillow walloped him in the face. It split open, filling the room with clouds of feathers.

THUMP! CLUMP! BIFF! BOFF!

They flopped back on the sofa out of breath.

"Phew," panted Bertie. "That was great. What shall we do now?"

He found the remote and switched on the TV. *This is the life*, thought Bertie. Mum and Dad never let him watch telly this late. And there were so many great programmes he wanted to see. He flicked through the channels. A love story – yuck! A cookery show – boring! A quiz show, adverts, more adverts, a horror film… WAIT! Bertie never got to watch scary films.

"Shall we watch this?" he asked.

"*Night of the Zombies III*. Wicked!" said Kevin. "It's *well* scary."

It turned out that Kevin had seen lots of scary films. It was the first time Bertie had heard him say more than three words.

They switched off the big light and settled down to watch the film.

It was midnight. The moon was out. The people in the house were all asleep. An eerie mist rose off the lake. Bertie sunk deeper and deeper into the sofa. He hugged his pillow.

He hoped there weren't actual zombies in this film.

THUD, THUD, THUD!

Bertie gulped. They were coming.

CRASH! A zombie's hand smashed through a window.

"YEAARRRRGH!" yelped Bertie, diving behind the sofa.

He peeped out. *The zombies were in the house. They walked like robots and had staring eyes. They were climbing the stairs to where the people were sleeping…*

Bertie chewed his fist. Why hadn't anyone warned him scary films were so … scary? Maybe he should go to bed? But if he went upstairs he'd never get to sleep. He would lie there all alone in the dark. And what if the zombies came to get him? He peeped through his fingers at the screen.

What was that? The room was suddenly dazzled with light. Two bright eyes beamed through the curtains like headlights. Wait a moment, they were headlights. A car was pulling into the drive. Help! This was worse than any horror film! Mum and Dad were back already!

CHAPTER 4

Bertie looked around wildly. The house looked like it had been burgled. The floor was a sea of crisp packets, biscuits and sticky chocolate wrappers. There was a wet patch on the carpet and beside it the remains of Mum's best vase. One of the pillows looked like a punctured football. White feathers had settled on everything like snow. Bertie felt a wave of panic. If Mum and Dad saw the house like this he was dead.

He shook Kevin by the arm. "Quick! They're back!"

"What?"

"Mum and Dad! We've got to tidy up!"

Kevin frowned. "You're blocking the screen! This is a good bit!"

Bertie couldn't believe it. Was Kevin just going to sit there and watch the film? This was a matter of life and death!

A car door slammed. Any minute now Dad's key would turn in the lock. There was no time to lose. Bertie flew round the room like a whirlwind. He hid the pillows behind the TV. He brushed feathers under the sofa. He righted the fallen lamp and mopped the puddle on the carpet with tissues. What else? What else? Mum's best vase! Bertie got down on his hands and knees and picked up the bits. He grabbed flowers and crisp packets and sticky wrappers.

THUD! THUD! THUD!

They were coming up the path! He rushed into the kitchen with his arms full. Quick, quick, where could he hide the evidence? The fridge! No one would look in there! He yanked open the fridge door and bundled everything inside.

RATTLE, RATTLE!

The key was turning in the lock. Bertie slammed the fridge shut and thumped upstairs in a blur of speed. Just in time! He burst into his room, dived under the covers and lay there panting.

"Kevin! We're back!" called Mum. "Was everything OK?"

Bertie listened with his heart pounding. A few minutes later he heard the front door slam. Kevin had gone. Bertie lay back and breathed a sigh of relief. It was a close thing, but he thought he'd got away with it. Mum and Dad hadn't noticed anything. He stole out of bed and crept on to the landing.

"Such a nice quiet boy," said Mum. "I hope he and Bertie got on all right."

"Well at least he's in bed," said Dad. "And the house is still in one piece. Do you want a bedtime drink?"

Bertie froze. No! How could he have been so stupid? His dad always made hot chocolate at bedtime. Hot chocolate needed milk. And milk was kept in the…

CRASH!
CLATTER!
SMASH!

"BERTIE!"

Dirty Bertie

LOO!

To Chris Newton and Heather Collins of the Scottish Book Trust - thank you for looking after me so well ~ D R

For Megan and Bethany with love ~ A M

Contents

LOO!

CHAPTER 1

"NO RUNNING!" barked Miss Boot, grabbing Bertie's arm as he flew past. "And that means you, Bertie. Get on the coach in an orderly fashion."

The class stampeded up the steps as Mr Weakly counted them on board. Bertie, Darren and Eugene elbowed their way past, trying to reach the back seat.

Bertie raced down the aisle and skidded to a halt. Know-All Nick, and his weedy pal Trevor, had got there first.

"Sorry, Bertie," smirked Nick. "No room!"

"Yeah, no room!" grinned Trevor.

"But *we're* sitting there!" said Bertie.

Mr Weakly came down the gangway, looking flustered. He was a nervous young teacher who Bertie had once locked in the store cupboard for a dare.

"Come on, boys," he sighed. "Sit down. We're waiting to go."

"But sir, they're in our seats!" complained Bertie.

"Yeah, they had the back seat on the way here," said Darren.

"Tough cheese! First come, first served," said Nick, smugly.

"Couldn't you all just share nicely?" pleaded Mr Weakly. He could see Miss Boot glaring at them like a black cloud.

Bertie pointed at the empty seat in front. "Oh, Nick, isn't that your money?"

"Where?"

"There – under the seat!"

Nick got up to look. "Where...?"

WHOOSH!

Bertie and his friends barged past him and hurled themselves on to the back seat, pushing Trevor out of the way.

"Sorry! First come first served!" grinned Bertie.

"Sir!" whined Nick. "They stole our seats! It's not fair!"

"NICHOLAS!" Miss Boot's voice shook the windows like a hurricane. "SIT DOWN, THIS MINUTE!"

Nick flopped sulkily into the seat in front. The coach set off.

Bertie stared out of the window.

The day had been one big let down. School trips were meant to be fun, but Miss Boot always chose something "educational". Why couldn't they go somewhere interesting – like a chocolate factory, or a space centre? Miss Boot's idea of a trip was to drag them hundreds of miles to the Costume Museum in Dribbleswick. Bertie had spent hours staring at dummies dressed in petticoats and frilly bloomers. Worse still, the museum shop didn't even sell sweets. He'd ended up buying a useless plastic ruler that said "I'VE BEEN TO THE COSTUME MUSEUM!" Bertie took it out of his bag and stared at it. Hang on, maybe he could find a use for it after all?

The back of Nick's head was poking up above the seat in front. Bertie reached out and prodded it with his ruler. Nick scratched his head.

PROD! PROD! Bertie did it again. Nick swung round.

"Was that you?"

"What?" said Bertie, innocently.

"I'll tell," warned Nick, turning back. Bertie bent back the ruler, taking aim.

THWUCK!

"OWW!" howled Nick, clutching his head. "Miss! Bertie hit me!"

Miss Boot spun round. "BERTIE! IS THIS TRUE?"

"No, Miss," said Bertie. After all, he hadn't touched Nick, the ruler had.

Nick narrowed his eyes. There was a long journey ahead. He would get Bertie for this.

CHAPTER 2

The coach crawled along slowly, nosing through traffic. Bertie felt like they'd been on it for a week. He had drunk the last of his lemonade while Eugene and Darren drew pictures of Miss Boot on the window. At long last they pulled off the motorway into a service station.

"We're stopping for fifteen minutes!"

boomed Miss Boot. "You will stay with me and Mr Weakly. And you will *all* be going to the toilet!"

The class filed into the service station with Miss Boot leading the way. They divided into two groups, with Mr Weakly taking the boys off to the men's toilets. But when they arrived there was a large notice outside:

CLOSED FOR CLEANING

"Oh dear! How unfortunate!" groaned Mr Weakly. "We'll try the café. Follow me, boys."

Bertie had had enough of staying with Mr Weakly. Besides, he didn't even need the loo. And he had spotted arcade games in the foyer.

"Hey, look," he whispered to Darren

and Eugene. "Let's stay here!"

"No!" said Eugene. "I need the loo!"

"Me too," said Darren.

"Fine," said Bertie. He hung behind as the others trooped into the café.

Ten minutes later, he'd shot down fifteen Vargon spaceships and reached level nine. But he'd started to squirm in his seat. Maybe he did need the toilet after all? Luckily, he still had a few minutes. He rushed to the café...

Nooo! The queue for the toilet stretched for miles.

Bertie looked for Darren and Eugene but they'd been and gone. He spotted Know-All Nick near the front of the queue. Normally he wouldn't have dreamed of asking Nick for anything, but this was an emergency.

"Hey, Nick," said Bertie. "Let me in. I really need the loo."

"There's a queue," said Nick.

"I know," replied Bertie. "But I can't wait. And the coach'll be going any minute. Please!"

Nick raised his eyebrows. "Ahh, poor Bertie. Are you really bursting?"

"Yes!"

"Would you like to go in front of me?"

"Can I?"

"No chance," snapped Nick. "Get to the back."

Bertie drooped to the end of the queue. Through the café window he could see Mr Weakly counting children on to the coach. The queue inched forward at a snail's pace. Nick came out of the toilet and hurried past.

"Don't wet your pants, Bertie!" he jeered.

Finally Bertie reached the front.

KERSPLOOSH! The toilet flushed. *Yes! My turn at last!*

But just as the toilet door opened, someone grabbed him by the arm and hauled him out of the café.

"BERTIE! Come *on*!" fumed Miss Boot. "EVERYONE IS WAITING!"

"But Miss, I need—"

"We are late! Back on the coach. NOW!"

Bertie's classmates cheered as Miss Boot frogmarched him up the steps. The driver started the engine and the coach pulled away.

Darren turned to Bertie. "You all right? You look a bit pale."

"I NEED THE LOOOOOOO!" wailed Bertie.

CHAPTER 3

Cars and lorries zoomed past. Bertie tried to count them to keep his mind off other things.

"Thirty, thirty-one, thirty-loo…"

It was no good, all he could think about was needing the toilet. How long would it be until they got back to school? He wasn't sure he could hold out much longer. His tummy ached. His hands were sweating. Why oh why hadn't he gone when he had the chance?

He nudged Darren.

"Darren, I need the loo!"

"I know, you already told me."

"But I REALLY need it. Like, now."

"You can't go now! There's no toilet on the coach!" said Darren.

"I know that!" groaned Bertie.

"So what are you going to do?"

"That's what I'm asking you!"

Eugene leaned over. "What's up?"

"Bertie needs a wee," replied Darren.

"What? A piddle?"

"A widdle."

"A tiddle?"

"SHUT UP!" groaned Bertie. "You're not helping!"

Darren and Eugene grinned. They were starting to enjoy this.

"D'you know what I do when *I* need to go?" said Darren. "I sing to myself."

Bertie sighed. "Don't be stupid."

"No, really! It works, doesn't it, Eugene?"

"Yeah," said Eugene. "It takes your mind off it. Go on, Bertie."

Bertie rolled his eyes. Still, he'd try anything if it stopped him thinking about what he was trying not to think about.

"All right. What shall I sing?" he asked.

"I know," said Darren. He whispered something to Eugene. They burst into song:

"*Does the driver want a wee wee?*

Does the driver want a wee wee?

Does the driver—"

"SILENCE!" thundered Miss Boot, jumping to her feet. "WHO WAS THAT?"

Know-All Nick raised his hand. "Bertie, Miss."

"It wasn't ME!" cried Bertie. "Honest."

Miss Boot glowered. "I have my eye on you, Bertie. Do not try my patience." She sat back down.

Darren and Eugene fell about giggling. Bertie scowled at them.

"How'd you like it if you were dying for the loo and all I did was make jokes?" he grumbled.

Darren shrugged. "If it's that bad, tell Miss Boot," he said.

"How's that going to help?"

"You never know, maybe she'll stop the coach."

Bertie doubted it. Miss Boot didn't like to be bothered on coach trips. She especially didn't like to be bothered by him. Nevertheless, he had to try.

He got up and began to make his way down the gangway.

"Where are you going?" asked Know-All Nick.

"Mind your own business," said Bertie.

He found Miss Boot marking a pile of books with a red pen.

Bertie coughed loudly. "'Scuse me, Miss, I, um … need the toilet."

Miss Boot looked up. "WHAT?"

"I need the toilet," said Bertie. "Badly."

Miss Boot snorted. "Go and sit down."

"But Miss, I can't wait…"

"Then why didn't you go at the service station like everyone else?" snapped Miss Boot. She stared accusingly at Mr Weakly.

"Oh dear!" he said meekly. "I thought they all did."

"I didn't have time!" moaned Bertie. "I was about to go when you made me get on the coach!"

Miss Boot sighed wearily. "Why is it always you, Bertie?"

Bertie didn't answer. He was hopping from one foot to the other like a morris dancer.

Miss Boot slammed her book shut. "Well, there's nothing I can do now. We're on the motorway. You'll just have to wait till we get back to school."

Bertie moaned. "How long will that be?"

Miss Boot looked at her watch. "About an hour."

CHAPTER 4

Bertie drummed his feet on the floor. He stood up, then sat back down. He squirmed. He wriggled. He bounced up and down in his seat.

"Do you have to?" sighed Darren.

"I can't help it! I need to goooo!" wailed Bertie.

This was torture. Agony. And the rain

wasn't helping. Large raindrops ran down the window. Drip, drip, drip. He felt like he was going to explode. It was no good. He would never last out. He stood up and began to shuffle down the gangway. Know-All Nick stuck out an arm to bar his way.

"Why can't you sit still?" he asked.

"What's it to you?" said Bertie.

"I know!" said Nick, smiling. "YOU need the toilet!"

"No I don't!" said Bertie, turning pink.

"Yes you do! BERTIE NEEDS THE LOO-HOO!" sang Nick at the top of his voice.

People were turning round. Bertie pushed past and hurried towards Miss Boot.

"Um, Miss?"

Miss Boot let out a long sigh. "You again? What now?"

"I still need the toilet. Desperately!"

"I told you before, you'll have to wait."

"I caaaaan't!" moaned Bertie, crossing his legs. "Can't we stop, just for a minute?"

"We're on the motorway!" barked Miss Boot. "Where do you suggest we stop?"

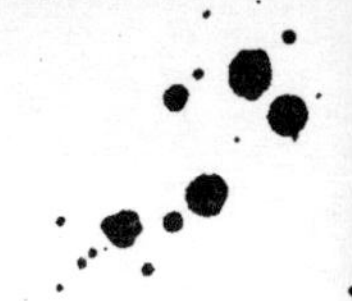

"At a service station!"

"There isn't another one. And stopping on the motorway is against the law. You'll just have to hold out."

Bertie whimpered. "I don't think I can!"

"You will."

"But what if I can't?"

Miss Boot groaned. "I don't know, go in a bottle!"

Bertie returned to his seat with the look of someone who was doomed. Still, Miss Boot had said it, and when a teacher told you to do something he assumed they meant what they said. And what else could he do? He rummaged in his backpack and found his empty lemonade bottle. He unscrewed the lid, checked that no one was watching and slid into the corner.

Then Bertie did it. The thing that would have made his parents blush with shame and his classmates howl in horror. A smile of huge relief spread across his face.

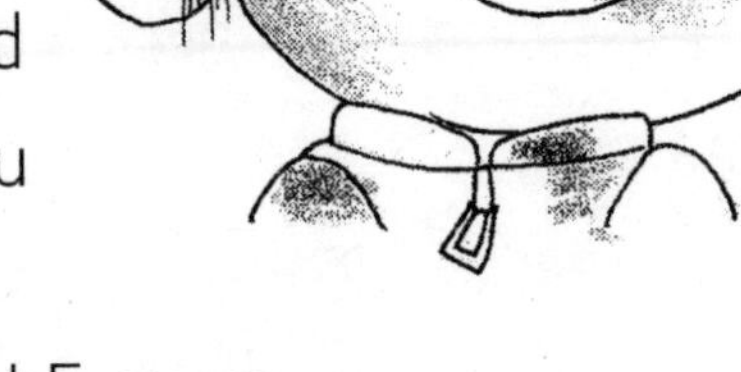

Darren looked over. "Ewww! You haven't?"

"What?" asked Eugene.

"Bertie's weed in a bottle!"

"YOU DIDN'T!"

"All right, keep your voice down," said Bertie. "Nobody saw, did they? Anyway, Miss Boot told me to."

He carefully screwed the lid back on.

Eugene pulled a face. "Yuck! What are you going to do with it?"

Bertie hadn't thought that far ahead. He couldn't sit there holding a full bottle of wee. Somebody might notice! He unzipped the pocket of his backpack and stuffed the bottle inside. He could dump it somewhere on the way home.

At four o'clock the coach pulled up outside the gates. Bertie had never been so happy to be back at school. He put on his backpack and joined the queue to get off. Know-All Nick jostled him from behind.

"Get a move on, slowcoach! I thought you needed the loo!"

"There's a queue, fat face," said Bertie.

He jumped down the steps and waited for Darren and Eugene on the pavement. Just as they were going a reedy voice behind them cried out, "Oh, Bertie! Look what I've got!"

Bertie turned round.

Know-All Nick was waving a plastic bottle. It wasn't! It couldn't be! Bertie checked the pocket of his backpack. ARGHHH! It had gone!

"I've got your drink, Bertie! Na na nee na naa!" jeered Nick.

"Crumbs!" gasped Eugene. "D'you think we ought to tell him?"

Bertie thought about it. "No, why spoil it? He'll soon find out if he gets thirsty!"

DIG!

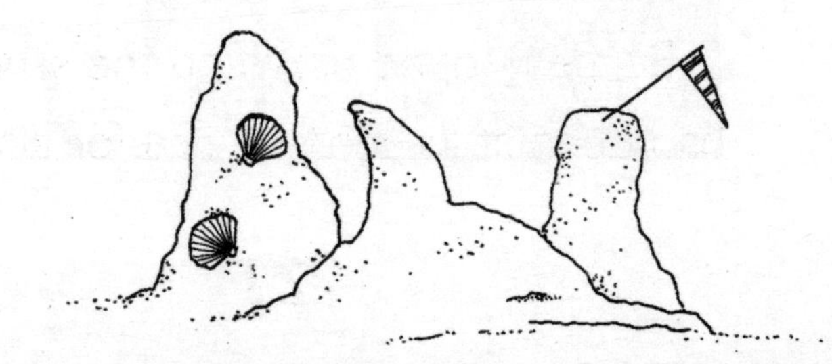

CHAPTER 1

"Mum, can I have an ice cream?" asked Bertie.

"No, you've just had lunch!"

"But I'm still hungry!"

"You're not hungry, you're just greedy. Now find something to do."

Bertie flopped down on the sand. They had been at Slopton-on-Sea for almost a week and he had done everything there was to do. It was okay for his parents – they *liked* doing nothing. And Suzy could lie around doing nothing for hours. But Bertie wanted to play. He stared at the windswept beach and the grey sky. If only Darren or Eugene were here – then they could play football, or pirates … or maybe pirate football.

Suddenly Mum got to her feet. "Goodness, isn't that the Riches over there?"

Bertie turned to look. A couple were coming their way loaded down with rugs, bags and beach chairs. Trailing behind was a goofy boy with lank, fair hair. Bertie groaned. *Not Royston Rich! What's HE doing here?* Royston was in Bertie's class and Bertie couldn't stand him. He was the biggest boaster in the school. Whatever anyone had, Royston had one that was bigger, better and ten times more expensive.

"Good heavens!" cried Mrs Rich, raising her sunglasses. "Fancy seeing you!"

"Yes," said Mum. "I didn't know you came here on holiday."

"It's our first time," said Mrs Rich. "Gerald's sister has a house by the beach, doesn't she, Gerald?"

"Actually it's more of a villa," yawned Gerald. "What about you?"

"Oh, we've just rented a little flat," said Mum.

"Actually it's more of an apartment," said Dad quickly.

"And here's Bertie!" squawked Mrs Rich. "Isn't that super, Royston? You'll have a little playmate!"

"Super," said Royston, glaring at Bertie.

"Lovely," said Mum. "Bertie's been moaning that he's missing his friends.

Why don't you two run along and play?"

Bertie groaned. Play with Royston? He'd rather wrestle an octopus!

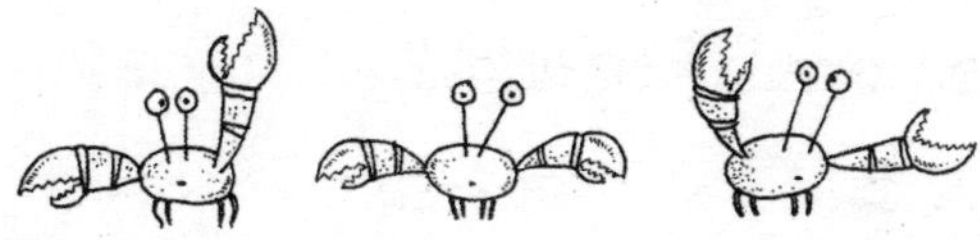

"So," sighed Royston, "what shall we do? Want to see my new remote control plane?"

"No thanks," said Bertie. "I'm busy."

He picked up his spade and began digging the hole he'd started earlier.

"That's rubbish!" sniffed Royston. "Why don't you make it bigger?"

"I *am* making it bigger," scowled Bertie.

"Your spade's too small. Why don't you get a better one?"

Bertie went on shovelling sand. He would have liked to bury Royston up to his neck.

"I'm getting a new bucket and spade for the competition," boasted Royston.

Bertie stopped digging. "What competition?"

"The sandcastle competition, stupid. Didn't you know? There's a prize and everything."

Bertie's eyes lit up. A sandcastle competition? With a prize? Why hadn't anyone told him? In Bertie's opinion, he was brilliant at building sandcastles.

"When is this competition?" he asked.

"Tomorrow," said Royston. "Maybe you should enter so you can watch me win.

I already know what I'm going to make and it'll be *miles* better than yours."

"Want to bet?" said Bertie.

"Suits me." They shook hands.

"See you tomorrow then!" said Royston, swaggering off with his nose in the air.

Bertie watched him go. He would teach that goofy-faced show-off how to make a sandcastle. Wait till tomorrow, then they'd see who was best!

CHAPTER 2

That evening, Bertie's family ate supper back at the flat. Whiffer hovered beside Bertie's chair hoping he would drop some chips on the carpet.

"Dad," said Bertie. "Can I enter a sandcastle competition? They're having one on the beach tomorrow. Royston reckons he's going to win."

"Huh! I bet he does!" said Dad. "We'll see about that."

"His dad's buying him a new bucket and spade," said Bertie.

"Typical," said Dad. "We'll get you a new one in the morning."

"That's not fair!" grumbled Suzy. "What about me?"

Mum rolled her eyes. "Aren't you taking this a bit seriously? It's only a sandcastle competition! It's meant to be fun. What does it matter who wins?"

"Of course it matters!" said Dad. "I'm not letting Gerald Rich's son win."

"Why not?"

"Because he's a smelly-pants show-off!" answered Bertie.

"Exactly," said Dad. "Anyway, we're bound to win. We just need to think of something clever."

"WE?" said Bertie.

"Yes, me and you. We can be a team."

Bertie's mouth fell open. "But it's a children's competition!"

"Don't worry," said Dad. "I'm not going to interfere, I'll just be there to offer advice."

Bertie had heard this before. When his dad offered advice it usually ended with him taking over completely. Like the time he'd helped with Bertie's history project and had stayed up half the night making an Egyptian pyramid out of yoghurt pots. Bertie didn't want to be the only boy in the competition who'd brought along his Dad. It would be so embarrassing!

Dad stroked his chin. "The question is what to make? It's got to be something eye-catching. What about the Houses of Parliament?"

"No!" groaned Bertie.

"Or the Eiffel Tower?"

"No!"

"Or an airport with planes and runways and a control tower..."

"NO, NO!" cried Bertie. "Dad, I'd rather do it by myself. Please."

Mum patted Dad on the arm. "Maybe Bertie's right. You come shopping with me and Suzy."

"Okay!" sighed Dad. "I'm only trying to help you win."

"It's not the winning that counts," said Mum. "It's the taking part."

Bertie said nothing. Anyone could take part. He wanted to *win*. But if he was going to beat Royston he needed a good idea. Everyone would be making crummy old sandcastles; his entry had to be something different. Something no one else would think of. He glanced down. Whiffer was still eyeing his chips with his tongue hanging out. That was it! Of course! Instead of a sand-castle he'd make a *sand-dog*! It was different, it was original and best of all he could get

Whiffer to act as his model. Bertie sneaked a chip off his plate and dropped it on the carpet. That prize was as good as his!

CHAPTER 3

Next morning Bertie arrived at the beach with his brand-new bucket and spade. Whiffer trotted eagerly at his heels. It was a bright, breezy day, with a few grey clouds out to sea. A large crowd of children had turned up for the competition. Bertie noticed many of them had brought shells and flags and other stuff to decorate their sandcastles.

"You're sure you don't want us to stay?" asked Dad.

"No, it's okay," said Bertie. "Whiffer will keep me company."

"Can we go to the shops now?" moaned Suzy.

Mum glanced at the sky. "It looks a bit cloudy," she said. "You better take my umbrella just in case. We'll be back for the judging. Good luck, Bertie," she called, as they headed off.

Royston Rich pushed his way through the crowd. Like Bertie he had a brand-new bucket and spade, though his were big enough to dig to Australia.

"Hello, Bertie! Come to watch me win?" he smirked.

"In your dreams," said Bertie.

Just then Mr Rich appeared. Bertie stared. He was carrying a new bucket and spade too.

"Wait," said Bertie. "Your dad's not entering – is he?"

"Oh yes, didn't I mention it?" said Royston. "Parents are allowed to help – it's in the rules. Luckily my dad's *brilliant* at making sandcastles."

Bertie glanced around. It seemed everyone else was here with their mum, dad or grandma. He was the only one entering by himself! He looked for his dad, but it was too late – he'd already gone. That two-faced rat Royston. He'd done this on purpose!

A large square of sand had been roped off for the competition. A woman wearing huge baggy shorts stood on a box to address everyone. She had a whistle round her neck and a clipboard in her hand. Bertie thought she looked like Miss Boot's ugly sister.

"You have one hour to complete your sandcastles," she barked. "When time is up I shall blow one blast on my whistle, like so. PEEEEP! That means put down your buckets and spades, immediately. I will come round with the other judges to inspect your work. Any questions? Splendid. Then on my whistle, begin!"

Everyone began digging furiously. Parents drew lines in the sand while their children stood by looking baffled. Royston and his dad were digging like slaves and had already produced a mountain of sand. Bertie, meanwhile, was trying to get Whiffer to pose.

"Sit boy! Sit!" he ordered. But Whiffer was too excited to sit. There was nothing he liked better than digging.

"SIT!" yelled Bertie.

He wrestled Whiffer's bottom to the ground and began to dig. Whiffer barked joyfully and bounded over to help. He kicked up showers of sand in all directions. Bertie sighed. So much for using Whiffer as a model! He'd just have to work from memory.

He set to work as Whiffer ran back and forth, leaving a trail of paw prints over a dozen sandcastles. Bertie pretended it wasn't his dog.

Forty minutes later, he stopped to wipe the sweat from his face. Building sandcastles was hard work. The grey clouds had drifted closer. The woman in baggy shorts passed by.

"Ah!" she said. "That is … hmm … well, what is it?"

"It's my dog," said Bertie. She was obviously blind as a bat.

"Really? Good heavens! Is there something wrong with him?"

"No," said Bertie, glancing round for Whiffer. He caught sight of him halfway up the beach chasing a flock of seagulls.

"Never mind, keep at it!" barked Baggy Shorts. "You've only got five more minutes."

She marched off, checking her watch and glancing at the dark sky.

Bertie took a step back to inspect his work. Even he had to admit it hadn't turned out quite as well as he'd hoped. His sand-dog looked more like a melting snowman. One lumpy blob stood on top of a bigger lumpy blob. The top one could have been a head but it was hard to tell. The nose was squashed, one eye had fallen off and the paws stuck out like a pair of mud pies.

Bertie turned to check out the competition. He stared boggle-eyed. Some of the other entries were amazing! There were playful dolphins, tiny sea horses and fairy castles covered with pink shells. Next to him was a

mermaid with seaweed hair. And best of all was a speedboat so real that it seemed to be skimming the waves. At the wheel was a goofy boy in a sailor's cap. Royston Rich. He caught sight of Bertie and waved.

Bertie's shoulders drooped. There was no way he was going to win. Royston's speedboat would walk it. And for the next million years he'd have to endure his endless boasting at school.

By now a crowd of people had gathered to watch. Bertie spotted his parents among them. They had rescued Whiffer, and Suzy was trying hard to stop him running off again.

Big black clouds blotted out the sun as Baggy Shorts climbed on to her box and blew a blast on her whistle. PEEEEP!

"Time's up!" she barked. "Everyone put down your—"

But her words were drowned out, as the clouds burst and the rain came pouring down.

CHAPTER 4

Everyone fled. Children dropped their spades and ran. Bertie's family ran too, finding shelter under the roof of the Beach Café.

"Where's Bertie?" asked Mum, suddenly.

Dad stared. "I thought he was with us!"

Suzy shrugged her shoulders. "Don't ask me, I was holding Whiffer but he ran off."

They peered through the pouring rain. The beach was empty apart from one large yellow umbrella. Under it they could just make out a boy and a dog sitting next to a shapeless lump of sand.

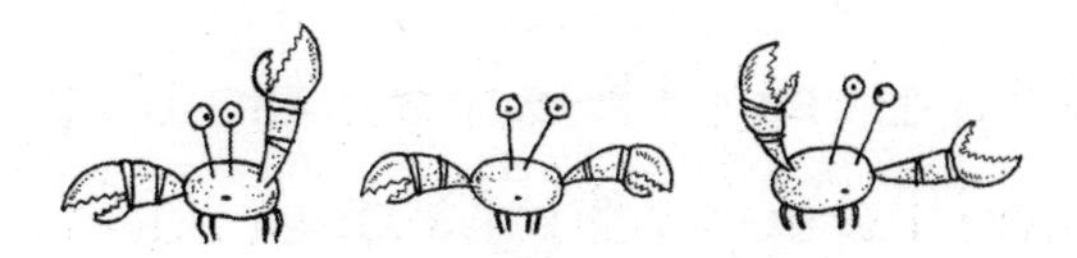

At last the rain stopped and everyone crept back to see what was left of the sandcastles.

The beach looked like a battlefield. The mermaid was a clump of seaweed, while Royston's speedboat was a soggy heap. Everywhere lay messy blobs of sand which had once been dolphins or sea horses.

The judges huddled together for a moment and Baggy Shorts climbed back on to her box.

"I regret to say the competition has been cancelled," she said. "The rain has ruined everything. There's really nothing left we can judge."

"Yes there is!" Everyone turned round. It was the boy with the dog.

"Look," shouted Bertie. "It's all right! I kept it dry!"

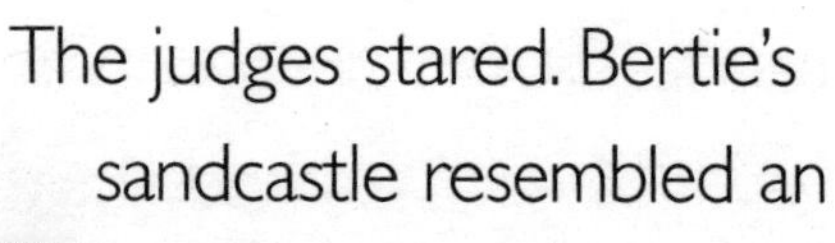

The judges stared. Bertie's sandcastle resembled an alien from the planet Blob. Nevertheless, it was the only entry left. They mumbled together, and finally Baggy Shorts turned to face the crowd.

"I'm pleased to announce that we have a winner. First prize goes to, um..."

Bertie whispered in her ear.

"To Bertie for his … er … unusual portrait of a dog. Well done!"

Bertie stepped forward to receive his prize. It was a giant hamper stuffed with cakes, sweets, toffee apples and goodies. As he carried it off he passed a goofy, red-faced boy throwing a tantrum. Bertie gave Royston a cheery wave.

Victory had never tasted so sweet!

MOVE!

CHAPTER 1

Bertie was watching TV when Mum and Dad burst into the lounge.

"Great news!" beamed Dad, excitedly.

"We're getting a hamster!" cried Bertie.

"No, better than that, we're moving house!"

Bertie almost fell off the sofa.

"MOVING?" he gasped. "When?"

"As soon as we've sold our house," said Dad. "It's going up for sale next week. Isn't that marvellous?"

"But I don't want to move," said Bertie.

"Where would we live?" asked Suzy.

"In Poshley Green," said Mum. "It's a much nicer area and we've already seen a house we like!"

"But I don't want to move!" grumbled Bertie, raising his voice.

Mum took no notice. "It's got a lovely long garden and a park over the road. And wait till you see the size of your bedroom, Suzy."

"Cool!" said Suzy.

"BUT *I* DON'T WANT TO MOVE!" yelled Bertie, jumping up and down.

Mum sighed. Dad frowned. "How do you know?" he said. "You haven't even seen the house yet."

"I like *our* house," said Bertie. "It's got my bedroom and all my stuff."

"Well you can take your stuff with you," replied Dad.

"And I'm sure you'll make lots of new friends," said Mum.

"What for?" asked Bertie. "I've got friends already."

"I mean at your new school."

New school? Bertie stared. Had they all gone raving mad? This was an outrage! A disaster! He had been going to Pudsley Junior practically all his life! It was HIS school! He could walk there from his house, meeting Darren and Eugene on the way. He didn't want to go to some horrible new school where the teachers had you flogged for breathing too loud in class.

"Well I think it'll be nice," said Suzy.

"No it won't!" scowled Bertie. "It'll be horrible!"

"Just 'cos I'll have the biggest bedroom!" crowed Suzy.

"No you won't, smelly-pants!"

"Will!"

"Won't!"

"Stop squabbling!" cried Mum. "I'm sorry, Bertie, but Dad and I have decided and we're going. I'm sure once you've settled in you'll love it."

Bertie slumped back on the sofa and turned up the TV. It wasn't fair! Nobody asked if *he* wanted to move. Why were parents always ruining his life? Well they could move if they liked but he wasn't going. He would lock himself in his room and never come out. Ever.

...Except to order pizza.

CHAPTER 2

A week passed and nothing more was said about the move. Bertie hoped Mum and Dad had forgotten the idea. But on Friday afternoon he was walking home from school with his friends when he spotted something in the window of Floggit's estate agents.

"That's MY house!" said Bertie.

"Wow!" said Darren. "Looks like your mum and dad are really serious."

Bertie pressed his nose against the glass.

"This is terrible!" he said. "We've got to stop them!"

Darren shrugged. "What can we do?"

"Maybe no one will buy it," said Eugene, hopefully.

They walked on in gloomy silence. Bertie couldn't imagine living somewhere without his friends. If they moved he probably wouldn't *have* any friends.

"Couldn't you put them off?" said Eugene.

"Who?"

"The people buying your house. Tell them it's falling down or something."

Bertie shook his head. "They'll see it's not falling down."

"But Eugene's right," said Darren. "All you have to do is put them off!"

"How?" said Bertie.

"Easy! Tell them you've got vampires living next door."

"Tell them there's a body buried in the garden!"

"Tell them it's got fleas!"

"It's a house, not a dog!" said Bertie.

All the same, maybe Eugene had a point. He couldn't stop his parents selling the house, but maybe he could stop anyone from buying it! It would just take a few unpleasant surprises.

Back home, Bertie got out his Top Secret Notebook and began to draw up his battle plan.

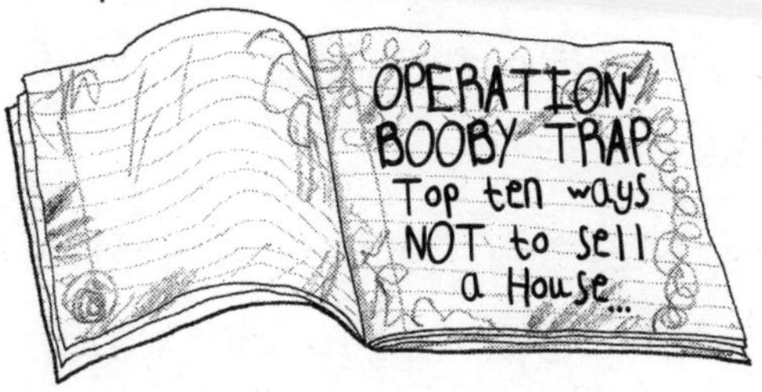

This was war.

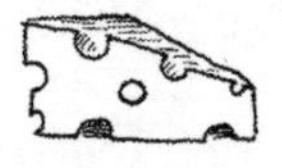  

Monday arrived. The first people to view the house were due at four and Mum was getting frantic.

"Bertie, have you tidied your room?"

"Yes!"

"And picked up your socks?"

"Yes!"

"And thrown away those rotten apple cores?"

"Nearly!" shouted Bertie. Bertie had never seen his house looking so clean and tidy. Mum had swept and polished till it shone like a palace.

DING DONG!

Enemy attack. Bertie hurried downstairs. Operation Booby Trap was under way.

"Now remember," said Mum, "stay out of the way and don't touch anything. What's that you've got?"

"Where?"

"Behind your back."

Bertie brought out a box. "Nothing. Just rubbish I'm throwing out."

"Hurry up then," said Mum, rushing to open the door.

"Mr and Mrs Mossop? Do come in! Shall we start in the lounge...?"

Battle stations! Bertie darted into the kitchen and closed the door. Setting the box down, he removed the lid and peeped inside.

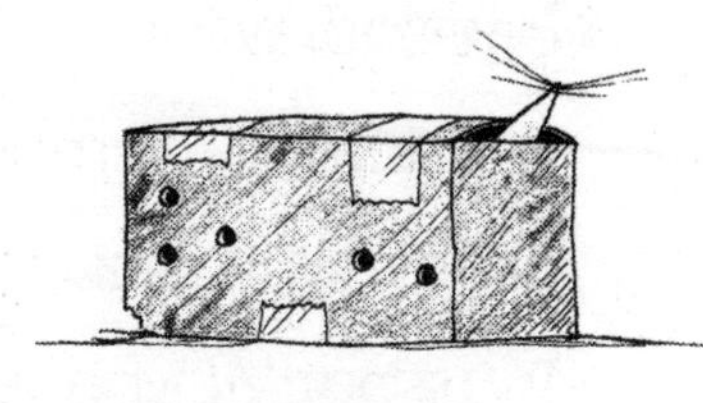

"Time to come out!" he whispered.

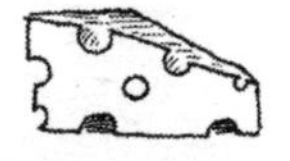  

Mum had finished showing the Mossops downstairs. Now for the bedrooms. She hoped Bertie had tidied his room.

"And this is my son's bedroom..." she said, opening the door.

Bertie looked up from the book he was pretending to read. He was slightly out of breath.

"Bertie, this is Mr and Mrs Mossop," said Mum.

"Pleased to meet you," smiled Bertie.

"What a nice quiet boy," said Mrs Mossop. "And doesn't he keep his room tidy?"

"Er … yes," said Mum, giving Bertie a suspicious look. She closed the door.

Bertie listened as they went downstairs. *Any second now*, he thought.

"ARGHHHHHHH!" Mrs Mossop burst from the kitchen. "MICE!" she shrieked. "You've got MICE!"

"I'm so sorry!" said Mum. "I can't think how they got there! Please don't go … maybe you'd like to see the garden?"

"No thank you!" bristled Mrs Mossop. "We've seen quite enough!"

The front door slammed. There was a heavy silence.

"BERTIE!" yelled Mum. "I want a word with you – NOW!"

Bertie crept downstairs. Mum was waiting for him with a face like thunder.

"All right, where did you get them?"

"Get what?" said Bertie.

"The mice. One of them ran up Mrs Mossop's leg!"

"Mice?" said Bertie, sounding amazed.

"I wasn't born yesterday, Bertie. The truth. *Where* did you get them?"

Bertie gulped. "Well … um …

I might've been looking after a couple of mice for Eugene. But I left them in their box."

Mum ground her teeth. "Listen to me," she said. "We are selling this house whether you like it or not. So you are not to bring mice, spiders, flies, beetles or any other creatures indoors. Do I make myself clear?"

"Yes," nodded Bertie. He tripped upstairs to his room and closed the door. Plan Number One had worked like a dream. It was a pity about spiders though because they were next on his list.

CHAPTER 3

The week passed. Visitors came and went. Mostly they went quickly as Bertie was lying in wait for them. He left taps running, muddy marks on walls and bars of soap where people could tread on them. Mum despaired. Dad threatened to stop his pocket money.

On Friday, Mum filled the dishwasher

and mopped the floor. No one had told her selling a house was so exhausting.

DING DONG! The Warners had arrived. Bertie was busy watching TV.

"Bertie, turn that off!" ordered Mum.

"But I'm watching *Alien Arthur*!"

"You can watch it later. And don't forget what I said – no more tricks!"

Mum rushed off to answer the door. Bertie heard voices in the hall and a small boy trooped into the lounge, followed by his mother.

"This is Mrs Warner and little George," said Mum.

George sucked his thumb and stared at Bertie.

"Why don't we start in the back room," said Mum.

Bertie waited till they'd gone and sprang into action. Time for Brilliant Plan Number Eight.

Dashing to the kitchen, he filled Whiffer's bowl with doggy chunks and took it upstairs. Whiffer was dozing in his favourite spot on the landing. When he smelled the food he followed Bertie eagerly. Bertie opened the door of the airing cupboard.

"Good boy! In you go!" he whispered, placing the bowl inside. Whiffer jumped in and Bertie closed the door. Now for Phase Two. He took out Suzy's mobile and rang his home number. The phone downstairs began to ring. BLOOP! BLOOP! That should keep Mum busy for a while.

A moment later Mrs Warner popped her head round Bertie's door.

"Okay to look round?"

"Fine," said Bertie. "Did she warn you?"

"Sorry?" asked Mrs Warner.

"Oh, nothing!" Bertie went back to his book.

"Warn me about what?" Mrs Warner persisted.

"The house. You do know it's..." Bertie lowered his voice, "...*haunted*?"

"HAUNTED?" Mrs Warner turned pale. George sucked his thumb. Bertie hit the REDIAL button on Suzy's phone.

"It's okay," said Bertie. "Usually he visits at night."

"Who?"

"The ghost!"

"Good heavens!" gasped Mrs Warner.

"It's my dog," Bertie explained. "He died last year, but now he's haunting us."

"You poor child!" Mrs Warner picked up George. "You've actually seen this ghost?"

"Oh yes!" said Bertie. "But mostly you hear him. You know, scratching and howling and so on. I expect you'll get used to it."

Mrs Warner looked worried. She didn't want to get used to it.

"Shhh!" Bertie held up a hand. "You hear that?"

They listened.

SCRATCH! SCRATCH! SCRATCH! Whiffer had finished his food and was pawing at the cupboard door.

"It's him – the ghost!" whispered Bertie. Mrs Warner held George tighter.

THUMP! THUMP!

"Oww oww owww!" whined Whiffer.

"That's it," gasped Mrs Warner. "We're leaving!"

They rushed downstairs and bumped into Mum in the hallway.

"You're not going?" she said.

"We couldn't live here!" said Mrs Warner. "Not with that awful dog!"

"Oh. You mean Whiffer?" said Mum.

Mrs Warner looked at her. "You've seen him too?"

"Well of course!" laughed Mum. "I see him all the time. He lives here."

Mrs Warner stared at her in disbelief. "You're mad," she said, "mad!" and fled out the door.

Mum caught sight of Bertie watching over the banister. She narrowed her eyes.

"What was all that about?"

"Search me!" said Bertie. "I'll just … um … go and check on Whiffer."

CHAPTER 4

Sunday morning. Bertie was fixing himself a snack. Dad was taking Suzy to her dance lesson. Mum hoovered the hall, dusted the mirror and tripped over Bertie's shoes. She stuffed some roses into a vase on the kitchen table.

"Flowers?" said Bertie.

"They make the house smell nice.

We've got people coming."

"Not again!" moaned Bertie.

DING DONG! Dave and Debbie Sweetly had arrived.

Mum took a deep breath. She wasn't sure she could stand much more of this. She hurried to the door.

"And Bertie," she said, "I'm warning you … BEHAVE!"

Bertie thought quickly. So far Operation Booby Trap had succeeded in driving the enemy out. But he was running out of ideas. How was he going to get rid of these people? He stared at the roses in the vase. Of course! People wanted houses that smelled nice. They didn't want houses that smelled disgusting! What he needed was something that really stank. Something so pongy you would smell it through the whole house. Bertie looked out of the window. Whiffer was nosing in the flower beds. He squatted down behind a bush. That could only mean one thing… An idea began to take shape in Bertie's head. No, he couldn't. He daren't. On the other hand, this was war. He fetched the pooper scooper and hurried outside.

CREAK, CREAK!

Bertie sneaked up the stairs balancing a lump of dog poo on the pooper scooper. Now where to hide it? Somewhere for maximum stink effect. The bathroom? His mum and dad's bedroom? Of course – Suzy's room!

Downstairs he could hear the Sweetlys talking in the lounge. He'd have to move fast. Bertie opened Suzy's door and slipped inside. His eye fell on her jewellery box on top of the bookshelf. No one would ever dream of looking in there!

A minute later the Sweetlys came upstairs.

"I love it, don't you, darling?" gushed Debbie. "It's got tons of space and … ohh!" She wrinkled her nose. "Can you smell something?"

Dave sniffed. "Oh… Eugh! Yes I can."

"It smells like … well … um…" Debbie turned to Mum. "Is your toilet blocked?"

"I don't think so," said Mum. She sniffed. There *was* a nasty smell.

"Why don't I show you the main bedroom?" she said, quickly.

But Dave was heading for Suzy's room. "I think it's coming from here!" he said, opening the door.

The smell was overpowering. They reeled back, holding their noses.

"UGH! It stinks!" gasped Debbie.

"It's horrible!" moaned Dave. "Where's it coming from?"

"I've no idea!" said Mum. "It's my daughter's room. Normally it smells of nail varnish!"

Mum looked under the bed. Dave looked on the shelves. Debbie opened Suzy's jewellery box.

Inside was a ghastly brown blob.

"Oh! Ohhhhhh!" screamed Debbie.

"Come on, darling, we're going," said Dave, grimly.

THUD! The front door slammed.

Bertie waited in his room for Mum to shout his name. Silence. He crept slowly downstairs. Mum was in the kitchen, talking on the phone.

"Yes … I see… Well thanks for letting us know."

"Who was that?" asked Bertie.

"The estate agent," said Mum, wearily. "The house we wanted to buy has been sold."

Bertie's face lit up. "Does that mean we're not moving?"

Mum sighed heavily. "Okay. I give in. I don't think I can take any more of this."

Bertie danced round the kitchen. He'd won! They were staying! Wait till he told his friends!

The front door banged. Suzy was back. She thumped upstairs.

Uh oh, thought Bertie. *I hope she doesn't go in…*

"ARGHHHHHHHHHH!"